STARFLEET ACADEMY

THE GEMINI AGENT

by Rick Barba

FIC
T
Starf

Simon Spotlight
New York London Toronto Sydney

ISBN 978-1-4424-1961-2 (hc) ISBN 978-1-4424-1342-9 (pbk) ISBN 978-1-4424-1426-6 (eBook) Library of Congress Control Number: 2011926957

Contents

CH.1.13
Gemini Away

The war is coming, thought Nverinn wearily.

As always, it would be fought by the young.

The old would plan and start the war, of course. But the young would fight it. The old would make the stirring speeches and rattle the swords, but the young would do the dying, sucked through breached hulls into the void of space.

Nverinn tr'Rehu could not fathom how anyone could doubt these facts: war coming likely within a decade, and thus the imperative of aiming the attention of the Star Empire's laser on the young. Both sides would send their ranks into hell's mouth. The best of those warriors, the ones who would turn the tide—whether Romulan or Federation—well, right now the males could barely grow facial hair, and the females were only recently capable of bearing offspring.

In ten years these young would be in the front ranks.

Everything would depend on them.

His desk workscreen beeped. Nverinn, deep in thought, stared down at the call icon that popped up on-screen. He considered ignoring it, but after a few seconds he reconsidered and tapped the screen.

"Yes?" he asked.

"I have the senator for you," said a voice through the desk speaker.

Nverinn tapped the screen again and a window opened.

"Hello, Nverinn," said the face that appeared. Her mane of graying hair was still a remarkable thing. Most Romulans, like Nverinn, had dark black hair. Tashal had been gifted with a head of beautiful warm brown hair that she was secretly very vain about. It framed her face like a luminous aura.

"Tashal," said Nverinn. "How are you, friend?"

Tashal smiled, though her eyes did not. "Not well," she said.

Nverinn nodded and then said, "You have bad news for me, I expect."

"Well, not entirely," said Tashal.

The Romulan Senate, the military High Command, and the Tal Shiar intelligence agency—the three-headed imperial leviathan—had been revisiting Romulan force tactics for years, preparing for what everyone knew was an inevitable reengagement with United Earth and the Federation. There was so much talk of the humiliation at

Cheron nearly a century ago spawning new tactics and technology. But so very little talk of the young warriors who would fight the next war.

Nverinn was just a scientist, but he had longtime allies in all three branches of leadership. Senator Tashal was one of them. He'd known her for more than fifty years. They'd once been lovers, but that seemed like two lifetimes ago.

"I managed to get approvals for your project," said Tashal.

At this, Nverinn sat bolt upright. This was entirely unexpected.

"What!" he exclaimed.

Tashal's eyes widened.

"Yes," she said. "But there is one disturbing condition, courtesy of our friends in Tal Shiar." After an extended pause, she added, "You're not going to like it."

"Tell me," said Nverinn. As he spoke, he tapped at his workscreen, opening up several more windows. Soon he had half a dozen data apps arrayed across the desktop. "I can activate Gemini on a moment's notice. Literally, at the tap of a button."

"I know," said Tashal.

"Gemini is already in place, with a full cover story. We're absolutely ready to go," Nverinn continued eagerly.

"I know that, too."

"Then what is it?"

"The condition is this," said Tashal. "One test agent may be activated."

"Vorta Vor!" exclaimed Nverinn eagerly. "I have only one agent ready to release!"

But the senator sighed. "Please allow me to finish," she said. "That is not the condition I was referring to."

Nverinn stopped dragging open data windows and looked into Tashal's eyes. They'd once been dazzling, bright as supergiant stars. But years of wearing a political mask, of infighting and intrigue and war planning, had left them darkened and wary and—when her guard was down, like now—openly sad.

"Once the agent has run its course," said Tashal, "it must be wiped clean."

Nverinn was shocked into silence.

The senator nodded for emphasis. "Terminated," she said grimly.

Nverinn slumped in his chair. He gripped the armrests and his own eyes began to well up.

"It must be done for the Empire," said Tashal quickly, and then she tapped the monitor, ending the conversation and disappearing from the screen.

This confirmed what Nverinn already knew: Tal Shiar was monitoring this conversation.

"Yes," he said. "For the Empire."

CH.2.13
Wunderkinder

Nyota Uhura was in heaven.

Or the geekish xenolinguistic equivalent of heaven, anyway.

The young cadet stood in the entry portal of one of the most locked-down locations in all of Federation space. Arrayed before her was a cluster of workstation pods that harbored a treasure trove of Starfleet's highest security voice data on the Romulan Star Empire.

And here was Uhura. At age twenty, she was just a first-year cadet, yet already one of Starfleet's most accomplished experts in all three Romulan dialects.

Adding to the exceptional quality of this moment was the close proximity of her escort.

"Welcome back, Commander Spock," said the datamaster at the check-in desk, an older gentleman named Dirk Galloway. He sported an English accent. "Always a *ripping* pleasure to see you, sir."

Spock smiled slightly and leaned forward in a bow.

"Professor Galloway," he said crisply, "this is Cadet Uhura. We spoke of her."

"Ah, the wonder child," said Galloway, rising from his chair and extending his hand.

Uhura's eyebrows rose, and she felt a wave of heat flow up to her face.

"Good to meet you, sir," she said, shaking his hand.

"My, and *lovely*, too," said Galloway. "Spock, you said she was brilliant, but you didn't say she was lovely. Or maybe you did. Did you?" He grinned mischievously.

Spock was slightly rattled for a fleeting moment. But he recovered quickly.

"Well, Professor," he said after a second, "I believe it is against Starfleet regulations for superior officers to notice such things."

Galloway nodded sagely.

"Ah yes, protocol," he said. "We'll just stick to brilliant, then."

Chuckling, the datamaster led Spock and Uhura across the room to a touch-screen workdesk. The entire wall in front of it was a tinted window that overlooked the central plaza of the sciences complex.

"Here, Cadet," he said. "Please use this wireless head-set for security purposes." He nodded at several people working at nearby desks, including a beautiful Vulcan female cadet at an adjoining station. He added, "It also provides a more pristine quality of sound."

Spock watched as Uhura picked up the feather-light headset from its desk cradle.

"I will be sending you select recorded samples," said Spock. "You can translate orally, but please type a transcription into each sound file's data box as well." He pointed at a message box on-screen. "As I explained before, these are actual combat recordings, Cadet Uhura, taken from Romulan pilots and ship's personnel in the heat of battle."

"Understood," said Uhura.

"Some of what you hear may be disturbing," cautioned Spock. "It is likely you will hear Romulans suffering injuries, perhaps even fatal ones."

Uhura nodded. "Understood, Commander Spock," she said.

Spock looked her directly in the eyes. She could see his concern for her.

"We have had these recordings for nearly a century, but this is a new analytical approach to Romulan tactical chatter," said Spock. "We aim to get a sense of their warrior ethos, their persona in battle." His look was penetrating; she held it steadily. "We want a sense of their culture and of their individual natures. In essence, Cadet, we want a deeper understanding of what Romulans are as a species, how they function, how they process information under fire. We want to learn more about *who* they are."

Galloway grunted. "Yes," he said darkly. "So that we can kill the bastards faster and better when they come at us again."

Spock noted Uhura's reaction and then said, "Professor Galloway's family was nearly wiped out in the Romulan attack on London in 2159."

"I'm sorry," said Uhura.

"Ninety-six years ago, I know," said Galloway. "I wasn't born yet, believe it or not. Nor were your own grand-parents, I daresay." He shook his head. "But any so-called sentient species that employs the incineration of civilian population centers as a method of war is, well . . . I'll stop now before I say something that makes me sound unchari-table."

Uhura just listened.

"Which, of course, I am," added Galloway with a wink as he attempted to lighten the moment.

Uhura didn't want to point out what she saw as the obvious irony: that humans had perpetrated some of the most indiscriminate civilian attacks in the history of war-fare. But she could see the pain on the professor's face and hear it in his voice, and she felt compelled to say something.

"Professor," said Uhura, suddenly touching his hand. "I grew up in an Africa not so far removed from wars of genocide and ethnic cleansing. I have older relatives who've passed on unspeakable tales that cannot be forgotten, nor should they." Now she squeezed his hand. "So I think I understand."

"My, my," said Galloway, glancing at Spock. "She *is* remarkable, isn't she?"

Spock tilted his head.

"If we can better understand the Romulan mindset, Professor Galloway, it is true, we may find tactical or psychological advantages to exploit in the next war," he said. "But a better discovery might be a way to *avoid* the next war, would it not?" He looked at Uhura. "Because the next war could very well conclude with some form of mutual, assured destruction . . . the Federation locked in a death spiral with the Star Empire."

Uhura's eyes gleamed as she listened. She'd always sensed something amazing at Spock's core—tendrils of Vulcan logic entwined with a distinctly Human sensibility, all wound into an unpredictable and fascinating tangle. She'd seen him inch close to the edge of emotion on a few occasions during classroom discussion. It was definitely in there: the edge of emotion. It made him far more interesting than anyone she'd ever met.

But underneath it all Spock had something even more interesting to Uhura. He was what her father, Njuktu, would have simply called "a good man." What Njuktu meant by that compliment was *not* simple, and it was his highest praise. It was something Uhura always looked for in people: fundamental decency, and the courage to stand by it. Spock had them both.

"True," said Galloway with a begrudging nod, bringing Uhura back from her musings. "Another war like the last could set back galactic civilization a thousand years, I suppose."

"And that would open a power vacuum that could be filled by something far more unpleasant and far less civilized than the Romulans," said Spock with impeccable logic. "At least, based on our limited knowledge of Romulan culture." His eyes widened a bit. "And to improve that end, we have Cadet Uhura."

Uhura suddenly felt more necessary than ever before in her life.

"Yes, then follow me, Commander," said Galloway, giving the Vulcan's shoulder a brisk collegial pat. "Let's not waste this cadet's time! I'll show you to the secure pod." He winked at Uhura, adding, "I do hate to take him from you, but Mr. Spock needs hands-on access to those transmission databanks."

"I'll survive," said Uhura with a grin.

"Are you quite sure?"

Uhura and Spock both spoke at the same time: *"Quite."*

This elicited a chortling laugh from Galloway that quickly evolved into a cough as he led Spock away.

Uhura slipped the headset over her ears, adjusted the mouthpiece mike, and moved her fingers into position over the touch-screen keyboard. As she waited for Spock to get situated, she gazed out the tinted window.

That's when she spotted the barefoot running boy again.

Who is that? she wondered.

The barefoot running boy, as few at the Academy yet knew, was Pavel Andreievich Chekov. Like Uhura, he was a wonder child. Except he was closer to being an actual child than your average cadet. At fourteen, Chekov was the youngest in the first-year class by more than five years. Most freshmen cadets were at least twenty-two.

Chekov was running because he planned to be the youngest cadet in history to win the annual Starfleet Academy Marathon. The previous youngest winner was eighteen.

And he was running barefoot because he was smarter than most cadets.

Chekov checked his run timer.

"Ay, Pavel," he muttered. "No good."

Today was Tuesday, his heavy mileage day; he'd been doing interval training over Golden Gate Park trails for almost two hours. As he cut across the residential quadrangle toward Nimitz Hall, his dormitory, he passed an outdoor basketball court where a few upperclassmen were playing a brutally competitive facsimile of the game.

"Hey, kid," called one of the players, a huge muscle pile from Alabama whose head sat like a cinder block on his shoulders.

Chekov slowed to a jog and nodded warily. He was used to older students asking him for help with their advanced theoretical physics. But Chekov suspected this fellow couldn't get within two lifetimes of a physics class.

"Listen, man, I canceled my *Chronicle* subscription," said Alabama as Chekov approached. "Why is it still coming?"

Now Chekov stopped, looking confused. "Excuse me?" he said.

"Why is the *Chronicle* still coming to my room?"

Chekov shrugged. "I honestly don't know," he said.

Some of the other players chuckled.

"Aren't you the paperboy?" asked Alabama.

Now Chekov smiled brightly. He whacked the big fellow in the arm. "That's a good one!" he said.

The other players laughed.

"I want that subscription halted, boy," said Alabama with a sharp-toothed smile.

"Consider it done," said Chekov. He turned and then jogged back to his dorm.

A lifetime of fending off bigger, older bullies had given Chekov some skills in doing so. He was born good-natured, and that helped. He had supportive, loving parents back in Russia, just outside Saint Petersburg, where he grew up an only child. He began showing gifted qualities and a stunning proficiency in mathematics at age four. As a result, Pavel spent the next decade of his life as the youngest, smallest, and smartest kid in a series of increasingly elite Russian and then international schools.

Now he was the second-youngest freshman cadet in Starfleet Academy history.

As Chekov passed two female cadets in the hall leading to his room, one reached over and tousled his hair. All the girls treated him that way— It was like having dozens of big sisters. Some were even fiercely protective of him.

When he reached his room, another upperclassman, a cadet named Fackler, leaned against the wall next to the door. He was one of Chekov's regular customers for math tutoring.

Fackler gave him a look. "What are you doing here, Pavel?" he asked.

Chekov smiled. "I live here," he said good-naturedly.

"Ah. Then where are your boots, kid?"

"Boots?"

Fackler looked annoyed. "*Gravity* boots?"

"I don't have gravity boots," said Chekov, frowning.

"Okay, well." Fackler clapped him on the shoulder and then walked down the hall. "Good luck, then."

Chekov waved his keycard over the scanner lock and the door whooshed open. His room was empty. Or rather, his floor was empty.

He stepped inside. Then he looked up. His furniture was inverted on the ceiling—arranged in exactly the same configuration as it had been on his floor when he left two hours earlier.

"Ay," said Cadet Chekov.

He ran a hand through his hair. Then he sat on the bare floor and started massaging his bare feet.

Dead week, he thought.

It was going to be just like they said it would.

● · · ✦ ·: · ✦ · ✦ ·· ·

Yes. Dead week.

Usually set in the final week of May, dead week was originally designed to be a quiet study period before the Academy's term-end examinations. But it had evolved into a week notorious for what the Cadet Handbook termed "stress-reduction activities."

And for good reason.

Two huge, life-changing events loomed just ahead for Starfleet Academy freshmen that week—well, three, actually, if you included cadets like Pavel Chekov, who sought to put their stamp in the Academy's athletic record book at the year-end Academy Games.

First, of course, came the exams—yes, important for *all* cadets, lower- and upperclassmen, but especially important for freshmen. Freshman term-end examinations marked the class's first major shakeout. Poor performers would be encouraged to explore options outside of Starfleet: in one of United Earth's planet-side military academies, for example, or in the Global Guard. This "encouragement" was very effective: The class could shed up to a fourth of its size after finals.

This fact was well known. Starfleet wanted it that way.

Meanwhile, freshmen anxiously awaited assignments for the second life-changing event: the annual Zeta Fleet Training Exercise. Technically, this two-day event—known simply as "Zeta"—was a component of term-end exam week; its official culmination. Yet Zeta was a separate proving ground. A freshman cadet's performance in the exercise was considered equally (if not more) important to his or her final exam results.

Zeta was a massive, fleet-size tactical combat exercise conducted in the Academy Flight Range near Saturn. Cadets were assigned to fully commissioned starships in active service, including ships of all classes: everything from two-man fighter crafts to mammoth ships of the line. These were then divided into two opposing fleets, Blue and Gold. Sometimes a third force was secretly deployed to introduce a surprise variable. Cadets were responsible for all aspects of ship operation, including navigation and weaponry. However, each onboard station had active-duty Starfleet personnel as overseers, ready to step in. This made for two days of crowded quarters. But a great deal of hands-on knowledge was passed down this way.

Riding massive tonnage into a high-stakes war-game scenario . . . mastering your onboard station . . . meshing as a crew . . . all the while knowing that your future in Starfleet depended on it—that was the easy part of Zeta. It was pure excitement. It was the reason many cadets joined Starfleet in the first place.

The hard part was waiting for the assignment list to be posted outside the Commandant of Midshipmen's office door.

Everybody knew that the plum positions in every Zeta exercise were on the two opposing Constitution-class heavy cruisers, the USS *Farragut* and the USS *Valiant*. Only the most promising cadets were assigned to these big boats. And the cream of the crop, the top two freshman cadets from the Command College roster, were assigned to the two captain's chairs for the *Farragut* and the *Valiant*.

So Zeta had everybody fired up.

You'd have to hate the very idea of spaceflight itself to not be excited.

CH.3.13
The Ambassador's Daughter

"Bones, you look sick."

Cadet James T. Kirk approached a figure slumped on a bench in the plaza near Hawking Hall. The four buildings of the Academy sciences complex were arrayed around this central square.

"Don't bother me, Jim," said the figure, raising his head. Medical Cadet Leonard H. McCoy, MD, looked miserable. He added, "I'm trying to enjoy breathing air while I still can."

Kirk grinned.

"Careful," he said. "If it gets to be too much fun, you'll want to do it all the time."

"Very funny," said McCoy.

Kirk sat down next to his good friend. With a sly look he said, "Say, did you know that they post the Zeta assignments on Friday?" He stared openly at three passing female cadets.

McCoy just glared at Kirk.

"You're over that aviophobia thing, right?" asked Kirk distractedly.

"You mean the fear of dying in something that flies?" said McCoy. "No."

"Ah, so that explains your surly demeanor."

"I'm always like this."

"True," said Kirk. "But today I sense . . . something more."

"I'm not happy about this damned Zeta thing," said McCoy.

Kirk nodded. "I figured."

McCoy waved his hands testily.

"Look," he said, "I've managed to make it through the entire first year without actually going *out there*." He looked up. "I hate space. The very concept of its *nothingness* gives me nightmares."

Kirk, eyes still fixed on the female cadets, suddenly leaned forward and frowned.

McCoy noticed.

"Something wrong, Jim?"

"I just realized I don't know those girls," said Kirk.

"So?"

"So I know *all* the beautiful girls."

McCoy glanced after the women. A thin smile spread across his face.

"Do you think they're Romulan spies?" he asked.

"It's very possible," said Kirk. "Maybe we should tail them." He grinned.

"Right," said McCoy. "The key word being 'tail.'" He slumped back against the bench.

Kirk turned to face him.

"Buddy," he said, "I'm worried about your focus and energy level. I'm going to need you functioning at full throttle on my bridge during Zeta next week."

"*Your* bridge?" said McCoy with a laugh. "Which one is yours?"

"Doesn't really matter," said Kirk casually. "*Farragut* or *Valiant*, I'll win regardless."

"Oh, I'm sure you will," muttered McCoy. "And those other thousand cadets in your fleet will be so grateful."

Kirk grinned again. "They'd better be," he said.

McCoy said, "What makes you so sure you'll get the chair on a big boat?"

"Bones, come on," said Kirk. "Look at my peers. It's going to be Tikhonov versus me, and everybody knows it." He leaned back on the bench, draping his arms across its backrest. "You *know* that Captain Pike and the brass want to see another showdown."

McCoy nodded.

"Yes, the faculty does seem to enjoy your little duels with Viktor."

Viktor Tikhonov was Kirk's bitter rival in the Command College. A rugged, even brutal competitor, Tikhonov was a truly formidable foe. Like Kirk, he was a natural leader. The big Russian seemed to get paired against Kirk in almost every classroom and simulator training exercise, which was surely no coincidence. Their teams had battled to a titanic stalemate in the Advanced Tactical Training scenarios earlier in the year, with Kirk's crew pulling out a narrow victory in the end.

"There's certainly a dark poetic quality to the notion of you and Viktor playing chicken in heavy cruisers," said McCoy.

"We've done it enough times in the simulators," agreed Kirk.

Kirk had great respect for his rival. He knew Tikhonov was the stronger man in the physical sense and was more relentless in pressing his tactical advantages. But Kirk had a knack for finding good people, building a team, and letting them work. He trusted his crew, and they responded with loyalty and undying effort.

"Look, nobody puts in more simulator hours than I do," said Kirk.

McCoy had to nod at that.

"And, Bones, nobody *loves* it like I do," Kirk went on. "It's only fair, right? I would eat, drink, sleep, and do everything else on a ship's bridge if I could."

Another female cadet walked past and smiled shyly at Kirk. Kirk smiled back and added, "Well, except for that."

McCoy blasted out a laugh.

"I'm not so sure," said the doctor with amusement. "I think you love that new starship even more than you love women."

Kirk's eyes glowed. The Command College had just acquired a bridge simulator for the USS *Enterprise*, a new Constitution-class heavy cruiser under construction at Starfleet's Riverside Shipyards in Iowa.

"Bones," said Kirk, getting animated. "When that girl is ready to fly in three years . . . I mean, have you *seen* her specs?"

"Yes, Jim, I have," said McCoy. "You keep showing them to me, remember?"

"The *Enterprise* will be Starfleet's flagship, my friend," said Kirk. "I guarantee you that. And I'll be aboard on her maiden voyage, even if I have to sneak on as a galley cook."

Suddenly he noticed a small wasplike insect hovering quietly near the ground, not far from the bench. McCoy saw it too. He pointed at it.

"What the hell is that?" he asked.

Without warning, Kirk sprang from the bench and then stomped hard on the thing. It made a sickening crunch. Then he picked up the crushed remains with his thumb and forefinger. Tiny wires and circuitry hung like entrails from the "bug."

"Gosh, will you *look* at that?" he said with a grim smile.

McCoy glanced up and spotted four big cadets crossing the plaza toward them.

"What's going on, Jim?"

"Not sure," said Kirk as the cadets approached. He raised his voice, then said, "Maybe these guys know. Hey, did you boys lose something?" He waggled the smashed device and held it up higher.

The lead cadet just stared and said, "Kirk."

"Yes?"

The cadet held out his hand. Kirk dropped the bug into it.

"Doesn't look repairable," said Kirk, shaking his head. "That's too bad, because I know how incredibly *expensive* those things are."

At this, all four cadets jumped Kirk. McCoy jumped right into the fray.

"What the hell?" shouted McCoy, ducking a punch. "Who are these guys?"

Kirk, grinning wildly, spun so he was back-to-back with McCoy. "Don't know, don't care," he cried. "I just know it's dead week, and I am *not* getting pranked!"

●　·　✦　∴　·　✦　·　✦　·‥　·

Yes, dead week.

Everything on the line.

Intensity so thick, you probably couldn't cut it with a quantum-resonator laser diode.

Hence, stress-reduction activities.

So far: Coordinated, campus-wide midnight screams on Monday. A full-fledged musical number by four snorting Tellarite cadets in the middle of a stellar cartography lecture. Campus statues of famous admirals dressed in lingerie stolen from an Orion cadet. Reversed peephole scopes on dormitory doors. Waterslides down residence hallways. A Ping-Pong gunfight carried out with insane tactical precision.

Parties. More parties. Parties ending in complicated sleepovers.

Plus the occasional fistfight.

● · · ✦ ∴ ✦ · ✦ ·· ·

"Take a break, Cadet Uhura," said Commander Spock through the headset.

Uhura took a slow breath. "Yes, sir," she said.

"That one was difficult, I am afraid."

"It was, sir."

"I have some cross-checking to do," said Spock. "Please shut down and then go get some dinner. I will meet you later in my office. We can review the transcripts."

Uhura smiled.

"Sounds good, Commander," she said.

Translating these recordings was indeed difficult, just as Spock had warned. Military intelligence scanners had picked up plenty of Romulan combat chatter during the Battle of Cheron, a decisive victory for United Earth. Like most people on Earth, Uhura had grown up with propaganda images of the pitiless Romulan "warrior"—always a foul, inhuman beast with a lust for blood. This was tempered a bit by Uhura's advanced studies of the Earth-Romulus War at the Nairobi Girls Academy. There she learned that Romulans made sensible, intelligent decisions after their defeat at Cheron. Indeed, their input into the subsequent cease-fire and Neutral Zone Treaty was not just reasonable, but even enlightened.

Still, the Romulan military had a reputation for ferocity and cold cruelty. So hearing the obvious confusion and fear and pain in the Romulan voices at Cheron was surprising, even heartbreaking at times. The pilots were young; many were female. They clearly had camaraderie. They cared for one another. Some sounded cocky; some calm and professional; some emotional, even elated; some nervous and unsure. But once their ships took damage and the void rushed into hull and cockpit and bridge, most of these Romulan voices just sounded terrified.

"Listening to ghosts?" said a voice just to her left.

Uhura plucked off her headset. It was the Vulcan girl at the next station.

"In a sense, yes," said Uhura.

"Well, you look haunted," said the girl. "Here." She handed Uhura a small bottle of spring water. "Take it, I brought a six-pack today."

"Thanks," said Uhura. She cracked the cap and then took a swallow.

"Thirsty work," said the girl.

"Are you translating too?" asked Uhura, nodding at the girl's workdesk.

"No, my stuff is much more mundane," she replied. "I'm analyzing hull scans. Not very exciting."

Uhura smiled. "I'm Uhura, first year," she said.

"T'Laya," said the girl, reaching out her hand. "First year also." As they shook hands she added, "Until they kick my butt out."

Uhura gave her an amused, skeptical look.

"Right," she said, glancing at T'Laya's security badge. "Sketchy types like you always get Level Four Alpha clearance around here."

T'Laya glanced down at the badge. "I stole this off a dead guy," she deadpanned.

Uhura laughed. She liked this girl. She clapped a hand over her mouth as other researchers in the room glanced or frowned at her.

"Sorry," she whispered with a wave.

"Anyway, you know what I mean," said T'Laya.

"Finals?"

"No *way*. I'll ace those."

Uhura nodded. "You mean Zeta, then," she said.

"I'm going to make demands," T'Laya said with a nod, a conspiratorial tone to her voice. "It could get ugly."

"You have Zeta demands?"

"See, my deal is, I won't fly on little spaceships," explained T'Laya. She pointed at her workscreen. "I spend all day identifying structural weak points where their hulls crack open. You wouldn't believe how many there are on a typical Romulan Talon-class scout."

"Fortunately, Starfleet doesn't fly Romulan scouts," said Uhura, grinning.

"Your ignorance is charming, Cadet," said T'Laya with a wink. "I promise you that every Starfleet scout and run-about and shuttle has at least seven hull points that I could easily breach with a single stray meteorite or photonic micro-torpedo."

"So that's why you'll fly only on *big* ships," Uhura concluded.

"Correct," said T'Laya. "If I don't get a spot on the *Farragut*, the Zeta assignors will have a big problem on their hands. They might need to take out a legal restraining order."

Uhura marveled at how funny this Vulcan girl was.

Vulcans weren't known for their senses of humor. She took a few sips of water and discreetly gave T'Laya a once-over. She seemed like the kind of girl who got exactly what she wanted. Smart, outgoing, funny. It didn't hurt that she was gorgeous.

"I don't want to sound racist," said Uhura, "but you seem awfully *peppy* for a Vulcan."

"No worries, I get that a lot," said T'Laya with a smile. "My father was an embassy guy," she explained, "so I spent very little time on Vulcan as a girl. My mother died when I was an infant and he never remarried, so I had a succession of nannies, all native to the planets where my father was assigned."

Uhura listened with great interest. So T'Laya was indeed a full-blooded Vulcan, yet she acted human. Uhura was fascinated.

"That's just . . . an *amazing* way to grow up," said Uhura. "Cultural crosscurrents like that, as a real part of who you are, how you were *raised*. Not just stuff you read or studied or even observed. It must give you a different perspective on a lot of things."

T'Laya shrugged.

"I guess," she said. "I actually spent my miserable teenage years here on Earth. We started at the Vulcan Embassy in Berlin. Then they reassigned Father to San Francisco."

"Where is he now?" asked Uhura.

T'Laya tapped at her screen. "He died when I was fourteen," she said.

"I'm sorry," said Uhura quickly.

"It's okay," said T'Laya. "It happened here. He died suddenly, from an embolism. I ended up getting placed with a Vulcan family over in Marin County. They were very *humanized*, I guess you'd say. So I had a very unusual upbringing for a Vulcan."

"Wow," said Uhura.

Her frankness was so unlike the standard Vulcan demeanor, Uhura thought. But it made sense.

"So the Zeta list goes up Friday," said Uhura.

"Yeah," said T'Laya.

Her Vulcan gaze darted rapidly over the images on her screen. She quickly expanded windows with thumb and forefinger, scanning entries with her odd micro-flitting eyes. Then she expertly dragged a few data bits into a save folder. She was amazingly quick and knew exactly what she was doing. Uhura was impressed.

"Well, good luck," said Uhura, tucking her headset back into its cradle.

"Thanks," replied T'Laya. "You too!" She paused for a moment and then added, "If I can't get the spot I want, then I'm going to find a *boyfriend* with the spot I want."

Uhura raised her eyebrows.

"Oh, I know what you're thinking there, Uhura. We're

Starfleet cadets. We're better than that, right?"

"Nothing wrong with boyfriends," said Uhura cautiously.

"Do you have one?"

Uhura paused. Then: "No."

"Same here," said T'Laya. "Anyway, we seek equal partners these days, not boyfriends, right?"

"Right," said Uhura.

T'Laya nodded in agreement. "Inferior works too," she said, tapping the screen again.

"God knows *that's* not hard to find," said Uhura in a low voice.

T'Laya laughed. It was funny and small, almost a giggle . . . and it struck Uhura that she'd never heard a Vulcan laugh before, despite knowing several at the Academy.

T'Laya said, "The only thing worse than inferior is superior."

"Superior males are insufferable," agreed Uhura. She glanced quickly over at Spock in his work pod. "Mostly," she said.

T'Laya's laser eyes caught Uhura's glance. She looked over at Spock.

"Commander Spock is a growing legend among my generation back home," she said. "Or so I hear."

Uhura stared at her. "Really?"

T'Laya nodded. "For generations, the top Vulcan

students just automatically matriculated into our Science Academy, without a second thought . . . or a first thought, for that matter."

Uhura tapped a button to close down her workstation, turning her full attention to T'Laya.

T'Laya went on. "The Vulcan Science Academy is legendary in this quadrant. I'd kill for the opportunity to study there."

T'Laya looked over at Spock again, who was oblivious in his soundproof pod.

"Right," she said. "And then Spock, the brightest mind of his class, turned them down cold. And he came to Starfleet." She turned back to Uhura. "Before Spock, that never happened. And now look at the last four Starfleet Academy classes."

Uhura nodded. *More Vulcan cadets every year.*

"Following the rebel genius," said T'Laya. She lightly patted her chest. "There's always a rebel inside, when you're young."

Uhura caught an undertone. "So is that why you're here?"

"You mean, like, stalking Spock?" said T'Laya with a sneaky grin. "Maybe. There is something very sexy about him, don't you think?"

Uhura focused on gathering her things.

"Seriously, though," said T'Laya. "Who are the Alpha

males at the Academy right now?" She asked this while continuing her remarkably fast, nonstop data-scanning activity.

"Do you have an implant?" asked Uhura, distracted. "I've never seen anyone scan so fast."

T'Laya's jittery dark eyes relaxed and turned to Uhura. It struck Uhura again that T'Laya was a beautiful girl.

"Tell me," said T'Laya. "Or else."

Uhura picked up her workpad and tucked it into the padded slot of her backpack. "I'll put together a list," she said dryly.

T'Laya smiled.

"I keep hearing about this guy Jim Kirk," she said. "I hear he's the golden boy of the class." She paused—then with a hint of a smile added: "And I've heard he's incredible-looking. Quite a few girls seem to know him."

Uhura just stared at her, surprised.

"Do you know him?" asked T'Laya. A slight uplift at the end of her question. The linguist in Uhura immediately read it: *faking nonchalance. She's interested in James T. Kirk.*

"Oh, come on," said Uhura. "Kirk? Really?"

T'Laya turned her stunning gray eyes to Uhura again. "Ah, so you *do* know him," she said.

Uhura nodded. "Well, sort of."

T'Laya just kept staring.

"We've worked together on a few things," said Uhura.

"Of *course* you have," said T'Laya with a sly look. "I'm sure you all hang out together in a Starfleet Wonder Pack." She glanced over at the datamaster, and now Uhura knew the Vulcan girl had overheard her introduction to Professor Galloway.

As Uhura shrugged at T'Laya, the Vulcan girl's eyes shifted to the window. Suddenly her dark eyebrows knitted together.

"Whoa, are those guys *fighting* out there?" she asked.

Uhura turned to follow T'Laya's gaze outside. Then her eyes widened in alarm.

"Good lord, it's Kirk," said Uhura.

"Which one?" asked T'Laya, squinting.

Uhura pointed. "That guy who just flew over the bench," she said.

"Ouch," said T'Laya, wincing.

Uhura jogged toward the security doors.

"Come on," she said. "Don't you want to meet your Alpha dream boy?"

A bright smile spread across T'Laya's face.

"Let's save him from those guys," she said. "Then he'll owe me one."

"Honey, there are two things wrong with that plan," said Uhura, pushing through the doors. "Kirk doesn't need to be saved. And Kirk definitely won't need to be in *debt* to you. He'll be happy to pay you back anyway."

CH.4.13
The Guarantee

Senator Tashal stepped off the shuttle.

"Greetings, Senator," said Nverinn, who stood waiting in the Center's docking bay.

"*Jolan tru*, Professor," she answered with a nod, using the more traditional Romulan salutation.

Tashal turned to the head of her security detail.

"Keep your team in the shuttle, Merak," she said. "I won't be long."

Merak bowed. "Very well, Senator," he said.

He turned and made a sharp gesture into the shuttle. Its door promptly hissed shut. Then he stepped up behind Tashal, just slightly to her left. As Nverinn led the senator across the bay, Merak stayed no more than five paces away.

Nverinn glanced back at the escort. "Impressive," he said to Tashal.

"I'm a senior senator now," she said.

Nverinn nodded.

"So you are," he said. "I hear you're a strong candidate for the open spot on the Committee as well." He smiled. "I feel unworthy."

The Continuing Committee was a small inner circle of the Romulan government comprised of select senators, ranking military officers, and high-level Tal Shiar intelligence operatives. The Praetor himself, head of the Romulan state, presided over both the Committee and the larger Senate. Although its formal duties were few, the Continuing Committee was a formidable power center in Romulan affairs.

"If I get the Committee spot, you *will* be unworthy," said Tashal with an amused sideways glance. "So enjoy my company now."

"I always do," said Nverinn.

"I have only until moonrise, Nverinn," she said, suddenly turning serious.

Nverinn nodded. "You'll stay for a full lunch, then?"

"Of course."

He led her down a corridor to an open atrium beneath a glass dome. The courtyard was meticulously gardened, and featured a colorful array of flora. A round table set for a meal was tucked beneath the drooping branches of a willowy tree.

Nverinn's research institute was in the Valley of Chula,

one of the most scenic regions on Romulus. His work over the years had been funded by generous grants from the Romulan High Command. Known as the Center, it was a first-class facility, well regarded. Nverinn himself had long been one of the most respected Romulan scientists in the Star Empire.

But Nverinn had never undertaken anything like his Gemini Project before.

"People are nervous about Gemini," said Senator Tashal as she sat. "The Tal Shiar, in particular. They consider espionage to be their exclusive imperial right."

"This I know," he replied. "And I certainly understand why."

A young girl approached carrying a crystal pitcher filled with sky-blue liquid, which she poured into two small beakers and then served. Nverinn and Tashal picked them up and clinked glasses.

"For the Empire," said Nverinn.

"If you say so," replied Tashal, glancing over at Merak, who stood a respectful distance away.

This amused Nverinn, and they drank.

Then Senator Tashal took a deep breath and leveled her eyes at the scientist.

"If Gemini succeeds, the Star Empire may owe you a debt that can never be repaid," she said. "But if it is detected, and the Federation can trace it back to us, then it may spark a war that Romulan forces are not yet ready to fight."

Nverinn nodded. "But the risk is worth it," he said.

"I agree," said Tashal. "So does the Praetor, by the way."

This made Nverinn brighten. "He seems like a sensible one," he said.

"He is," she replied. Her eyes darted uneasily. "*Very* sensible. Which is why I'm here."

Nverinn reached into a side pouch of his uniform and then extracted a small crystalline disk.

"The agent is fully active," he said. "Here, I've made a full report."

He handed the disk to Senator Tashal. But she didn't take it. He looked confused.

"Nverinn," she said. "You are a prizewinning scientist and a man of honor. We require no report."

He set the disk on the table.

"Then what do you require?" he asked.

"A guarantee."

Nverrin grimaced. "I can't guarantee success."

"That's not what we ask."

The young girl returned, this time bearing a platter of jumbo Romulan mollusks. She set it on the table, and then bowed with lowered eyes to the senator. But the girl couldn't help it— She raised her blue eyes to meet Tashal's. Tashal reached quickly to touch the girl's cheek. The girl blushed, then hurried off with a delighted smile.

"You're a hero to her," said Nverinn, smiling fondly after her. "More like a goddess, actually."

Tashal watched her go. "Her name?"

"Majal," said Nverinn. "She regularly points out that it almost rhymes with yours." They both laughed, and he shook his head. "She's only ten."

"Blue eyes," said Tashal. "Isn't that unusual for her race?"

"Extremely unusual," said Nverinn.

"And she's gifted like her sister?" asked Tashal.

"More gifted, I suspect," replied Nverinn.

Nverinn paused to spoon mollusks onto their plates before continuing. "Inbred ability gives her unprecedented control of the Gemini code. She becomes one with it, in essence. It's similar to synaptic pattern displacement, the phenomenon where a highly trained Vulcan can literally transfer his consciousness." He smiled. "These abilities are latent within Romulans, you know. We may master them someday."

"Perhaps," said Tashal.

The two sat in silence for a few moments, enjoying their meal.

Then Nverinn said, "What guarantee, Tashal?"

"If Gemini comes back to haunt us, you are working alone," she said. "You are a rogue scientist."

Nverinn tried to smile.

"Then, Tashal, my friend, I would be guilty of treason," he said.

"I suppose you would," she said, looking him in the eye.

"Then, more ale is required," he said, unable to hold her gaze.

He clapped his hands, three sharp raps. Within seconds the girl returned with the pitcher. Nverinn nodded toward her as she poured.

"Wouldn't it be ironic, Senator," he said, "if her counterparts at the Federation's fleet academy were just as gifted and beautiful and deadly as she is? What if they're just like her?"

Tashal smiled sadly. "That's what we have to find out. And if they are . . . then ten years from now, it will be a terrible war."

Nverinn drained his second beaker of ale.

"But imagine what might happen, Senator, if we trained them *all* to explore the universe in the name of peace and the pursuit of knowledge," he said. "What if every last one of our gifted young killers was a scientist and an ambassador instead?"

Tashal drained her second beaker too.

She said, "The moons should be in an iridescent phase tonight."

Nverinn stood up. The view from this atrium was

designed to be breathtaking. Across the great rift, basalt formations rose in obsidian swirls. Mesas layered in red and purple hunkered on the horizon. He could not imagine the possibility of this world ending, of the Valley of Chula on Romulus ever ceasing to be. But then, he was a scientist. He knew that in galactic time, this valley's existence was a blip, with his own lifetime eons shorter. He also knew that the Romulan punishment for treason was beyond unpleasant. He would be allowed an uncensored Right of Statement before the painful, public execution process began.

As part of his guarantee, Nverinn would say nothing.

The moons should be iridescent tonight, he thought.

"So, your time is short," he said.

"Yes," she said.

"I have something to show you, then," he said.

CH.5.13
First Infection

Crickets woke Kirk.

When he opened his eyes, he felt pain, nausea, his skin crawling . . . and he remembered nothing.

He could see stars above. Night.

Kirk closed his eyes again. His head was swimming in images, none of which made sense. First thought to emerge: *Where's McCoy?*

"Bones?" he called out.

He heard a rustling nearby, so he sat up. His head thumped like a phase cannon.

Kirk groaned. "Bones? That you?"

Sweat cooled on his face. His throat felt bloated. Kirk wasn't a big drinker like some cadets, the ones who couldn't process the pressure. But he knew how too much alcohol felt. This was not that feeling. Something wasn't right.

He heard rustling again.

"Who's there?" He pressed his hands into his throbbing forehead. "Please be Humanoid."

A dark figure pushed through foliage. It moved toward him quickly.

"Cadet Kirk?" called a female voice.

"Yes," called Kirk. "You're not a predator, are you?"

"No, Mr. Kirk," replied the dark figure now standing over him.

"Good," Kirk said, groaning. He lay back down. "Because I really need some rest."

A search lantern glowed in his face.

"You've probably been resting quite some time," said the woman.

Kirk shielded his eyes from the light.

"Just a few more hours," he said. "Let's talk tomorrow." He looked around him. "Are these flowers? Am I dead?"

A female face leaned down toward him. In the lantern's glow, it looked angelic.

"My god, I *am* dead," said Kirk.

"Why do you say that?" asked the woman.

"Because I'm clearly in heaven," said Kirk.

The angel rolled her eyes. She said, "We need to get you to a hospital bed, Cadet." She reached out a hand. "Get up if you can. They're waiting for you at the Medical College."

"Who?"

"Your friends," she said.

Kirk's eyes widened. "Friends?"

"Yes. I'll walk you there." She watched him for a second. "But can you walk? Or should I call a medical van?"

Kirk frowned. "I don't need a damn van."

Taking her hand, he staggered to his feet. He stood for a moment, staring at the woman. She was tall, almost his height. She appeared Human, but there was something exotic in her features that made Kirk wonder what race she was. Then Kirk noticed her black uniform and forgot about her race. Lieutenant bars, Starfleet Intelligence.

Kirk sat back down in the flowers.

"Maybe just another minute," he said.

As he lay back and things went black again, Kirk heard the woman flip open her communicator.

"Yes, this is Lieutenant Caan," she said. "I found him. I need a medical team in the flower garden outside the Shuttle Hangar. Now."

Kirk was suddenly flooded with memories of Iowa.

He floated up the old rock quarry wall. It seemed so real. He reached out to touch it.

The next time Kirk woke, he was in an ICU bed with an IV needle stuck in one arm and three wafer-thin biosensors taped to the other.

Above him, Dr. McCoy was waving a medical tricorder. Next to McCoy stood Cadet Uhura. And next to Uhura stood the prettiest Vulcan girl Kirk had ever seen.

Kirk looked at the girl and said, "Hi, I'm Kirk."

She squinted down at him and said, "You don't remember me."

"*Sure* I do."

McCoy rolled his eyes. He said, "Boy, does *this* sound familiar."

The Vulcan girl looked over at Uhura. "Wow. There's a punch in the gut."

Kirk reached for her arm. "I *want* to remember you. Believe me. I can't believe I'd forget meeting you . . ."

"Oh, I believe you," said the girl.

McCoy gently pushed Kirk's arm back down. "Don't disrupt the biosensor feeds, Jim." He glanced over at Uhura. "I think he'll be okay. Thanks for sticking around. You guys can go."

Uhura nodded. "Come on, T'Laya," she said. "Want to grab some dinner?"

Kirk tried to sit up. "See, I *knew* your name was T'Laya," he said.

Again, McCoy gently pushed him back down.

"I need clues!" said Kirk. "What happened? Give me clues."

Uhura looked down at him.

"Surely you remember *something*," she said.

"No!" protested Kirk. "Nothing! I'm a blank. Except . . . wait." He turned to McCoy. "Bones, were we fighting?"

McCoy grinned. He pointed at an abrasion over his own left eye.

Kirk looked upset. "I *hit* you?"

McCoy chuckled. "No, the other guys hit me," he said.

"Is that why I'm here?" asked Kirk. "I got my ass kicked?"

McCoy looked offended. "Jim, did you take a blow to the head? There were two of us and only four of them."

"T'Laya and I came to help, but you clearly had the situation under control," Uhura added dryly.

Kirk exhaled. "Good," he said.

McCoy leaned in to examine Kirk's eyes with a small flashlight.

"I'll fill in the gory details later," he said. "But in a nutshell: We had some fun with a few upperclassmen who had tried to put one over on you in some idiotic dead week prank. Then they left to go nurse their wounds and their egos, and the four of us"—he used his finger in a sweeping motion to indicate himself, Kirk, T'Laya, and Uhura—"decided to go grab a drink. But then you started acting like a lunatic. And then you disappeared. We all split up to look for you, with no luck."

"Was I drunk?" asked Kirk.

"No."

"What was it, then?"

"I have no idea." McCoy shook his head gravely. "But something happened to you, Jim. When they delivered you an hour ago, your tricorder readings were off the charts. Heart and metabolic rates sky-high, pupils dilated, shallow breathing, cold sweat. At first I thought you were having a damned heart attack."

"Maybe those goons slipped me a Mickey," said Kirk.

"I actually considered that," said McCoy. "But your system isn't having a drug reaction, according to these readings." He tapped on his medi-pad to download the latest tricorder data. "These are consistent with signs of a viral infection."

"So I'm just sick?" said Kirk.

"Maybe," said McCoy. "We'll know more when we get the blood results."

Uhura said, "Well, Kirk, gotta go. I'm glad you're alive."

Kirk pointed at her. "If I did anything to you that I can't remember, I'm sorry."

With a barely perceptible smile, Uhura said, "You were actually quite a gentleman before you vanished. Frankly, I was shocked."

"And, admit it . . . you were a little disappointed," said Kirk.

Uhura rolled her eyes, then turned to go.

"God only knows what happened *after* you vanished," she said. "I'm sure you left a trail of mayhem."

As the women turned to leave, Kirk called after them. "Why didn't I meet you before today?" he asked T'Laya.

T'Laya and Uhura exchanged an amused glance.

"Wait, there's no way I met you before today. . . . This is definitely the first time I've ever had memory loss," Kirk said.

"No, it's not that," T'Laya assured him with a grin. "It's just that you're consistent. . . . You said the same thing to me when we met for the first time a few hours ago."

And with that, the beautiful Vulcan gave him a quick wink, and then turned to leave with Uhura.

"That girl is amazing," Kirk said as he watched T'Laya leave.

But McCoy wasn't listening. He opened the valve on a drip chamber attached to Kirk's IV tube. "Jim, I'm giving you something to sleep," he said.

Kirk stared up at the ceiling. "How long was I gone, Bones?" he asked.

"About six hours," replied McCoy.

"Wow," said Kirk. "What did I do for six hours?"

"We'll probably read about it in the morning papers," said McCoy, amused.

Kirk closed his eyes. The medicine was fast acting.

He saw Iowa again. Swimming in the quarry with his brother, Sam.

And then Kirk was in deep, dark waters.

Midnight, three hours later:

McCoy sat at a desk near Kirk's bed in the ICU, angrily scrolling through lab reports on his medi-pad. Things weren't making sense. When things didn't make sense, McCoy got surly.

Then he glanced over at Kirk . . . and nearly slipped off his stool.

A gorgeous woman in a jet-black Starfleet uniform was leaning directly over his patient.

"Ah, excuse me, miss?" called McCoy. "This is a secure area. Are you authorized?"

She stepped toward him, flashing a holo-badge.

McCoy raised his eyebrows. "Wow, Level Six clearance," he said. "You must be a spook."

"I'm Lieutenant Caan," she said.

McCoy nodded. "How can I help you, Lieutenant?"

Lieutenant Caan pointed at Kirk.

"How is he, Doctor?" she asked.

McCoy held up the medi-pad lab reports. "Tough to say," he said. "He seems fine now, physically. But his blood work is odd."

"How so?"

The woman's eyes were bright aqua blue and unblinking, and McCoy found it hard to look into them without losing concentration.

"Pardon me for asking, Lieutenant," he said, "but why would Starfleet Intelligence be interested in this matter?"

"You're the attending physician?" she asked.

"Yes."

McCoy was amazed: still no blink. Eyes wide and watchful. And mesmerizing.

"And you are Leonard McCoy?"

"Yes."

Lieutenant Caan nodded, then turned to look at Kirk, who slept peacefully.

"You were in the patient's company earlier today, is that right?"

A small vein in McCoy's neck began to pulse. "Yes, that's right," he said.

"And you're good friends with Cadet Kirk?"

"Is this some kind of inquisition?" blurted McCoy. "Should I ring up my lawyer on speed-dial?"

Lieutenant Caan gave McCoy a bemused look.

"Dr. McCoy, I'm not a police officer," she said. "A lawyer would be of no use or consequence."

Few things irritated Dr. Leonard McCoy worse than breaches of medical ethics. One of those things was when

Starfleet functionaries tried to pull rank on him. So this was a double offense in his book.

"Look, you're in the intensive care unit at Starfleet Medical College," he growled. "This is holy ground. You're on *my* turf here."

Lieutenant Caan's aqua stare grew icy. She said, "Dr. McCoy, you *are* familiar with Starfleet Charter, Article Fourteen, Section Thirty-One?"

"Yes," said McCoy. "It's the Federation statute that supposedly lets you do whatever the hell you want in times of extreme threat." He pointed at Kirk. "Are you really pulling a Section Thirty-One on me here, Lieutenant Caan? Is this man an extreme threat?"

Lieutenant Caan slipped her security badge into a zip pouch on her uniform arm. "We don't know yet," she said. "But we have reasons to investigate. That's all you need to know at this point."

McCoy laughed loudly. "You'll have to give me more than *that*, Lieutenant, unless you plan an extraordinary rendition to torture me. Because last I checked, the Federation still honors doctor-patient confidentiality privileges."

Lieutenant Caan took a deep breath. Then she softened her tone.

"This is not a good start," she said.

McCoy said, "You can say *that* again. Look, Lieutenant,

Jim Kirk is my friend. I'm sure you people know everything about our backgrounds: our records, politics, exploits, associations, conquests, nights on the town. You probably have all our damn conversations recorded. But if you want medical information on my patient, you have to give me a bloody good reason for it. I'm not going to disregard doctor-patient confidentiality because you're feeling curious."

Lieutenant Caan nodded. "You're right," she said.

McCoy looked warily at her. She sounded sincere. But then again, she was a spook.

"Doctor, I found him," she continued. "He was in bad shape. I rode with the medical team." ·

McCoy sat back down on his stool.

"Ah, so *you're* the angel," he mused aloud before he could stop himself.

Lieutenant Caan narrowed her eyes.

"Pardon me?" she asked.

"Jim woke briefly about an hour ago," McCoy began to explain.

"Did he make a report?" she asked.

"I'm afraid he did," said McCoy. "In his drugged stupor he told me some insane story about a beautiful angel who rescued him from a flower bed." He looked her up and down and then met her eyes. Was it his imagination, or did she blush at the implied compliment?

"With all due respect, Lieutenant, you seem awfully young for an Intelligence officer. And since you're working alone, I have to assume this isn't a Section Thirty-One situation. More like, *Hey, let's send in the new kid. Let her get some experience.*"

McCoy could see he'd hit a nerve. Lieutenant Caan seemed to draw herself up taller. Her aqua eyes didn't give away much, but now they flashed a bit. She looked McCoy directly in the eyes.

"This is my first solo assignment," she said.

McCoy almost hooted out a laugh but managed to restrain himself.

"How old are you?" he asked Lieutenant Caan.

"Twenty-five," she said.

"My god, you're younger than me," he said.

"By exactly eight months," she said.

McCoy was enjoying himself now. "You've done your homework," he said.

Lieutenant Caan tilted her head a bit. "I always do my homework," she said.

"Yes, you strike me as that type," said McCoy. "So let's say we negotiate. Tell me why you people are interested in my friend, and I'll bring you up-to-date on the blood work."

Lieutenant Caan frowned. "Has Mr. Kirk had other episodes like this recently?"

McCoy folded his arms and said, "Sorry, Lieutenant. You first."

Lieutenant Caan sighed. Then she said, "Okay. Our Internal Affairs division recently received notice from your Academy's IT department of irregular activity on the internal network . . . activity that traces to the account of James T. Kirk."

She stopped. McCoy just waited. After a few seconds of silence, Lieutenant Caan finally blinked. McCoy took it as a small triumph.

"What kind of activity?" he asked.

"Search engine," said Lieutenant Caan.

McCoy laughed. "Surely you realize that term-end examinations are next week," he said.

"Of course we do."

"So what's unusual about a guy doing research as final exams approach?"

Lieutenant Caan smiled and then said, "If Cadet Kirk was conducting searches on Fleet Dynamics or Tactical Analysis or other Command College course material, I would agree with you."

"He wasn't surfing for, um, porn, was he?" McCoy asked, afraid of what the answer might be.

"No," said Lieutenant Caan.

"So what were his search topics?"

"Himself," she said.

"Himself?"

"Yes. Requests to hundreds of databases on the search topic of 'James Tiberius Kirk.' Then thousands more requests on various branch-off topics."

McCoy tapped on his medi-pad to bring up the lab reports.

"So is researching yourself illegal?" he asked. He shrugged. "Is it even suspicious? I mean, haven't we all done something like that at least once in our cyber-lives?"

Lieutenant Caan had to admit that it was neither. But the sheer volume of requests put Kirk on a watch list.

"Standard procedure," she said. "And then today . . ."

"Ah, I get it." McCoy nodded. "Cadet Uhura filed the missing person report with Campus Security, and it probably got cross-referenced with your watch list."

"Exactly," said Lieutenant Caan.

McCoy flipped his medi-pad so she could view the display.

"Here's the lab work," he said.

Lieutenant Caan frowned at it. "What does it mean?"

McCoy moved next to her and pointed to the screen. "Jim's blood shows signs of fighting off a significant viral-type infection. These antigen readings suggest that it was a very robust presence. It really pushed his immune system hard." He shook his head. "To be honest, with these kinds of results, it doesn't surprise me that you found him blacked out in a flower bed. In fact, I would have expected much worse."

She looked over at Kirk. "Is it contagious, this virus?"

"Well, that's the odd thing, Lieutenant. There *was* no virus." McCoy scrolled down to another report. "This blood scan shows absolutely nothing resembling an infectious agent. In fact, the medical tricorder and lab scans revealed nothing unusual or foreign in his bloodstream or lymphatic system." He tapped the window closed. "Nothing! Whatever caused the acute systemic response left without a trace. Or was never there in the first place."

Lieutenant Caan pulled out a small digital pad and jotted some notes. As she did, she said, "So to summarize: You're saying Cadet Kirk's body responded as if in reaction to a virus, but no sign of any actual virus can be found?"

"That's exactly what I'm saying."

"Thank you, Doctor," said Lieutenant Caan.

"You're welcome, Lieutenant."

She flipped her notepad shut. "I don't see much connection between Cadet Kirk's medical situation and his irregular online activities, do you?"

McCoy thought for a moment, then said, "None at all."

"To be perfectly honest . . . I don't expect much more to come of this," said the lieutenant. "But I have a report to file, so I'd appreciate any help or input."

McCoy walked over to Kirk's hospital bed.

"I'll send you my diagnostic notes after I finish updating the patient chart," he said.

"I appreciate that, Dr. McCoy. I'll be going now."

McCoy looked down at Kirk.

"Sleeping Beauty will be sad he missed your visit," he said.

The lieutenant cracked a smile.

"I expect he'll see me again," she said.

McCoy nodded.

"That should be a fun interview," he said.

Kirk rode down a dusty rural highway.

It looked very familiar.

He glanced down. His legs were pumping the pedals of his old red Photonic two-speed, the bicycle on which he spent most of his boyhood. It was the best feeling in the world.

Up ahead: a boy on another bike. A blue Photonic.

Kirk pedaled hard and caught up. It was Sam.

"Hey, Jimmy," said Sam.

The brothers rode side-by-side. Then Sam veered off the highway. A side road. Not a road, actually, but a make-shift lane created by vehicle tires. Kirk stomped on the brakes. The red Photonic shimmied and kicked up dust as it skidded to a halt.

"Come on, chicken!" called Sam, pulling away.

Kirk watched. Then he jumped hard on the pedals and followed.

He pulled even. The brothers rode side-by-side, again. Picking up speed.

"Chicken!" yelled Sam, grinning wildly.

Kirk grinned back. It was a race.

Up ahead, the vast quarry canyon opened up. Kirk pulled ahead. Then Sam pulled ahead. Both boys were flying toward the great precipice, a hundred yards ahead.

At the last possible second, as always, the Kirk boys hammered their brakes. Both bikes, red and blue, went into side skids, dust flying. Both stopped mere feet from the death drop.

Kirk, laughing, let out a howl.

Then Sam looked at him. His face was dark.

Kirk frowned. He suddenly felt afraid. "What is it?" he asked.

Sam said, "They're coming for you."

CH.6.13
Second Infection

The next day, Wednesday—"Zeta Minus Two"—Cadet Chekov sat at the workdesk in his spare, windowless closet in Nimitz Hall. He hummed a Prokofiev strain as he plotted warp coordinates on a 3-D galactic-map screen: a review exercise for next week's final exam. When he finished, he smiled widely.

"Course laid in, Captain," he said to himself.

He tapped an on-screen icon.

"Helmsman," he said, "you are cleared for warp factor six . . . no, wait." He slapped his forehead. "That's the *captain's* order, not mine."

For Zeta, Chekov expected to be at the navigator's station on a substantial ship, probably one of the heavy cruisers. He was the top student in his advanced stellar cartography class: The next cadet wasn't even close. But unlike most of the rest of the freshman class, Chekov would be perfectly happy to navigate for a Class F shuttle or a lowly supply transport. Starfleet status and the ship pecking order didn't matter to him. He loved the stars. Navigating them was his dream job. He didn't care for which ship.

He leaned back in his chair. It rested on the floor now, where it belonged.

All of Chekov's furniture was back in place, thanks to a few roommates (all female) plus a Campus Security officer with a hand phaser. Chekov's "redecorators" had thoughtfully used a nadion-sensitive polymeric bonding glue to stick stuff to the ceiling. Thus a simple cold phaser pulse (at weakest sub-one setting) dissolved the glue. Chekov and the girls then lowered everything back to the floor.

Situation normal again.

Then he heard a buzz. He looked down. His workdesk screen flickered.

Over on the wall, a hatch opened.

"Who is it?" called Chekov, standing up. "Who's there?"

He heard a loud suctioning sound as the room's robotic housekeeping unit emerged.

Chekov relaxed.

Ay, cleaning day, he thought.

The Academy dorms featured smart rooms. All room environmental functions were linked to the room's workdesk, so cadets could control lights, heating/cooling, sound, media . . . and even schedule the Robo-Maid unit to keep the floor clean.

"I thought I set you for Sundays," said Chekov as he examined his flickering workdesk screen. "Well, friend, I need to study today."

But when he tried to bring up the Room Environment Menu, the screen simply went blank. Chekov kept tapping. Nothing happened. As he leaned closer, he felt something jab his left ankle.

Chekov looked down.

The Robo-Maid was stabbing at him with its room corner attachment, trying to vacuum his legs.

"What are you doing?" he yelled. *"Ow!"*

The unit kept following him as he dodged around the room, so he went to the door and tapped the exit button. Nothing happened. He punched it a few more times. The door didn't budge.

"Oh, come *on!*" exclaimed Chekov.

The Robo-Maid latched onto his pants leg and wouldn't let go, so he pushed it away and then jumped up on the bed. Then he pulled out his communicator, hitting a speed-dial number.

"Residential Services," answered a voice. "Can I help you?"

"It's trying to suck me into the maintenance grid," said Chekov.

"Say that again, Cadet?"

"The cleaning robot is—"

Suddenly the tiny room's sound system burst alive, blasting music so loud that two speaker pods literally exploded. His other electronics went haywire too, beeping and ringing and buzzing and, in the case of the smoke detector, shrieking at ear-shattering decibel levels.

"My room has lost its mind!" yelled Chekov into the phone.

"Try a reboot," said the voice, sounding bored.

Chekov could barely hear the advice. He couldn't tell if the speaker was male or female or, as in the case of certain aliens, neither. The room noise was too loud to pick out subtleties.

"I tried that already!" he shouted. "The system is frozen. The door, too. I'm trapped in my crazy room!"

Now people were pounding on his door. Voices outside were drowned out by the room's cacophony.

"I don't know what to tell you," said the voice. "Maybe try turning everything off, then turning it all back on again?"

Chekov looked at the phone with disbelief. He took a deep breath, then said: "Is there a master power switch for the entire room?"

"I really don't know."

"Well, neither do I."

"I'm afraid I can't help you," said the phone voice. "We'll have to send a tech."

"How quickly can one get here?" asked Chekov.

"Probably tomorrow, or Friday."

"But I'm locked in my room!"

"Mmmm," said the voice. After a long pause it said: "I'll red-tag the request."

"What does that even mean?"

"Thanks for your call."

"Wait! How do I get out?"

"The tech will know what to do," said the voice.

Chekov cursed in Russian. Then the line went dead. He stared at his phone.

Now the Robo-Maid reversed its suction engine, spewing a gray cloud of days-old dust across the room.

"Ay . . . *stupid* maid!" yelled Chekov.

Coughing, he rushed around the room, trying to manually disconnect devices from power sources. Most were wireless and had no discernible on/off switch. Clearly, somebody had tampered with his settings. But how? His workdesk link was Starfleet-issued and the Academy's internal network was highly secure. Plus, Chekov, a wizard-level hacker in his spare time, had created his own supplemental firewall.

Yet this cyber-infection had slipped through all that in just seconds.

Chekov pushed his chair underneath the screaming smoke-detection module and angrily ripped it from the ceiling. It kept wailing in his hand. He hurled it hard into the wall. The ear-splitting shriek finally died.

He could hear his communicator buzzing now.

Chekov checked the incoming caller: Alex Leigh, his neighbor and a fellow navigator trainee.

"You okay in there, Pavel?" she said when he answered.

"Aye," called Chekov.

"Are you sure?"

"Yes, I'm fine," said Chekov. "The worst is over, I think."

As he said this, the automated fire suppression system activated. Water gushed from the sprinkler heads. Dripping wet in seconds, Chekov smiled and stared up into the downpour.

"This is almost comical," he said.

"We're outside your door, kid," said Cadet Leigh. "Open up."

"The door lock is stuck!" said Chekov. "The whole room is haywire. Nothing works."

"Come on, there must be a manual override on the door," said Alex. "Did you try—?"

"Residential Services, yes," said Chekov. "They're *idiots*."

"I'll call the fire department," said Alex. "Hang tight!"

"Will do!" said Chekov.

Unfortunately, his room was very small: It literally *was* a closet, a former storage space refitted as a single room because of the Academy housing crunch. Within seconds, water was inches deep on the floor. Chekov sloshed back to the workdesk, and he tried again to access the room controls, but no luck. The screen was frozen.

"I hate you," said Chekov.

Then a voice crackled through the speakers.

As Chekov stared, the display flickered alive and a figure appeared on-screen. The image was murky, but it was clearly a male in a cadet uniform. The figure leaned toward the camera.

He said: "Cold water is a bad way to die."

Audio effects distorted the voice. Chekov felt a small wave of panic.

He looked down. The water level was rising steadily.

"I'm a quarry rat," said the figure. He seemed to be slurring his words, but the audio distortion made it difficult to tell. "Quarry water goes down deep, forever, and it gets colder and colder. It's dark. Black. It's like death. I felt it. My brother felt it."

And with that, the display went black. Then Chekov's room lights began to dim.

"Oh no," said Chekov. He felt his chest and throat constrict as panic set in.

With a new sense of urgency, he dragged his desk chair underneath one of the sprinkler heads and then climbed up to examine it. As the lights grew dimmer and dimmer, Chekov tried to twist the head.

"Turn off!" he cried. "Off!"

The sprinkler head broke off in his hand. Now water shot from the pipe in a high-pressure stream. Chekov could still see in the darkness but only barely. Below him the water level in his tiny wedge of a room was rising more rapidly now, amounting to two feet deep.

He whipped open his communicator again and then called Alex Leigh.

"Where are the firemen?" he sputtered with a gasp when she answered.

"They'll be here," said Alex. "A cadet stuck in a room isn't exactly high priority, I guess."

Chekov almost lost it. "My room is filling up with water!" he cried.

There was a pause. Then: "You're kidding, right?"

"No!" said Chekov. "Can't you see it leaking?"

"I see nothing," said Alex. "Come on, Pavel. Don't mess with us."

The door must be watertight, thought Chekov. *Don't panic, don't panic.*

He tried to speak calmly. "The fire sprinklers are on," he said. "They're *gushing*, Alex. With tremendous force. The line pressure must be very high. The door is locked. The room has no window."

After another pause, Cadet Leigh said: "Oh my god."

"Yes, exactly," said Chekov.

"Call Residential Services again," said Alex. "We'll get back to the fire department." She barked an order to somebody else, then added, "Don't worry, Pavel. We'll get you out." Then she added, "This is ridiculous."

"Yes, it is."

"You can't *drown* in your own *room*," she said with incredulity.

"No, you wouldn't think so."

"We'll get you out," she repeated.

"Thank you," said Chekov.

He hung up, then dialed Residential Services. He looked down at the rising water. As he did so, the lights suddenly extinguished completely.

The room was now pitch-black.

Chekov felt icy cold water lapping at his feet. He put the communicator on speaker mode and then held it out. It gave enough light to see the water level rising over the seat of the chair where he stood.

"Residential Services," answered the voice. "Can I help you?"

"I certainly hope so," said Chekov. "First, let me just say that no matter what happens, I want my *full* room deposit back!"

CH.7.13
Room Service

The sound of wailing sirens sliced into Kirk's skull.

Above, two fire department hovertrucks flashed their emergency LED strobes, descending from the sky. Kirk had to cover his ears as he approached Yi Sun-Sin Hall, his dorm. A laser-bright landing circle beamed onto the ground in front of Nimitz Hall, the dorm directly across the quad plaza.

Kirk looked around for signs of smoke.

Behind him, a voice called out: "Hey, Kirk."

Kirk turned. "Beeker," he said. "What's going on over there?"

A towering Betelgeusian cadet emerged like a great unfolding stork from the Yi Sun-Sin entrance, gazing upward. His name was Bekkkr'esh Huuun'ivit, but most people just called him Beeker.

The bipedal avian Humanoid shrugged. "No idea," he said.

"Looks like something's going on over in Nimitz."

"Alcohol poisoning, maybe," replied Beeker. As he spoke, his separate eating mouth snapped sharply.

Kirk winced. "Dude, that's really *loud*, that thing you do with your tongues."

"Yeah, I know," said the Betelgeusian. "It's involuntary."

"Please clear the landing zone!" blared an amplified voice in the sky.

"Good . . . god," said Kirk, covering his ears.

The slow, aching walk home from the Medical College had been blissfully quiet. Kirk's head was still tender. His skin, too, had not returned to normal and it felt sensitized to the breeze and even to sounds, if that was possible. The whine of the descending fire trucks seemed to hurt everywhere.

"You don't look good, Kirk," said Beeker with a whistle, eyeing him sideways.

"I'm *not* good," said Kirk. He squinted in pain at the noise.

Beeker said, "Go rest awhile."

"Yeah, I'm going."

As Kirk shuffled down the hall to his room, other cadets rushed past him to check out the commotion across the quad. He waved his keycard over the door's scanner lock. When the door whooshed open, he staggered to his bed, falling on it with a relieved groan.

Thirty seconds later, there was a knock.

Kirk rolled over, determined to ignore whoever was at his door. The knock was louder the second time.

"Go away!" called Kirk.

The knocking continued.

Kirk sat up, holding his head. Then he went to the door. On the way he grabbed a hard carbon-fiber wrist brace left over from a touch football injury. Whoever was disturbing him was going to be sorry. He activated the door and raised the brace, planning to whack the unfortunate and persistent fool upside the head.

The door opened to reveal T'Laya. She was holding a bag in one hand and raising her arms up in mock surrender.

"If you hit me with that, I'll cry," she said.

Kirk lowered the brace. A slow smile spread across his face.

"Somehow, I doubt that," he said.

T'Laya held up the sack.

"Do you like Chinese?" she asked.

Kirk could smell the food. He hadn't eaten much in the past twenty-four hours. Suddenly, he was starving.

"I love Chinese," he said.

"Good," she said. "Because when I'm done eating, there might be leftovers."

Then she handed the bag of food to Kirk and strolled

past him, into his room. Kirk grinned. He reached for the wallet in his pocket.

"How much do I owe you?" he asked.

T'Laya sat on his bed and said, "You're deep in debt, pal." And then she patted the spot next to her on the bed.

Earlier that summer, when Chekov bought goggles and a snorkel in a Monterey Bay diving shop, he did it with plans to explore tidal lagoons around Santa Cruz. The last place he expected to use them was in his dorm room.

"I'm going down, Alex," he said, looking at his neighbor on his communicator's vid display. He pulled the goggles down over his eyes.

"Don't worry, my friend," she replied. "I hear the sirens outside."

"Not sure the fire department can do much," said Chekov. "I've been told Nimitz interior walls are built to withstand the initial shock wave and static overpressure up to six pounds–force per square inch in a standard airburst nuclear detonation."

Alex didn't answer for a moment. Then she said, "You are *such* a geek, Pavel."

Chekov nodded. "This I admit," he said.

"I got the hall maintenance director on another line," said Alex. "He's got his people closing the water main to the entire quad. Those sprinkler lines will shut down any second."

Chekov nodded again. "Affirmative," he said. "Thanks, Alex."

Alex smiled and then said firmly, "See you in a minute, kid."

The room was still pitch-black, and the water was almost chest-high now. Fortunately, Federation-issue communicators were waterproof—or supposed to be, anyway. Chekov would soon find out. After switching his phone display to its highest brightness setting, he hung it around his neck with a strap, facing out.

Next he pulled a vintage Red Army knife from a uniform pocket. He extracted its blade.

Finally he slid the snorkel into his mouth, waded to the door, and sat down.

The water was frigid, and the phone light wasn't very good. But now he knew exactly what to look for. Earlier, after twenty minutes of dead-end conversations with various so-called "tech" personnel at Residence Services, someone finally transferred him to the mobile link of an actual field repairman. In seconds the guy gave Chekov the precise location of the door's manual override mechanism. Naturally, it was at the very bottom of the door frame.

Breathing steadily through the snorkel, Chekov found the compartment, mostly by feel. It took just seconds to pry off its panel with his knife. But as he tried to dig under the latch that connected the door to the pneumatic air mechanism, the water level rose over the top of his snorkel.

He quickly stood, blowing hard to clear the tube. Then he ripped off the snorkel, held his breath, and was about to dive back down when his communicator beeped.

It was Alex. She wasn't smiling.

"News," she said. "Whatever malicious bug ate your local network also took out the building's network. They have to do a manual shutdown of the water system."

Chekov asked the obvious question left hanging in the air: "How long?"

"Nobody knows," said Alex. "Nothing like this has ever happened before."

"Ay!" cried Chekov.

"Kid, I—"

Chekov cut her off. "Gotta go," he said.

He inhaled and then sat. Just as the field tech had said, the latch was held in place by a single tungsten spring. He slid the blade under it and then pulled the knife handle, using it as a lever to lift the latch. It automatically released the door mechanism.

Gasping, Chekov popped out of the water.

"Yes!" he cried with an air punch.

He grabbed the door's recessed inner handle, trying to slide it open. He could feel slight movement, but there was too much friction in the door track. The water pressure was too great on the door.

He flipped open his communicator.

"Alex!" he called.

"Yes, Pavel," she said. "I'm here."

"Time to push!"

"Push what?"

"I've got the door on manual," he said. "But the water pressure won't let it slide."

"Ah, gotcha!" she said. "We'll push from this side for counterpressure while you yank it sideways."

"Exactly!" cried Chekov. "This is why I *like* you so much, Alexandra Leigh!"

She grinned, then turned from the screen. "Let's go, guys!" she yelled. "We're pushing against a thousand pounds of water, so dig in." Her command was so natural that, at that moment, Chekov was sure she'd be a starship captain some day.

He yanked at the recessed handle again.

At first the door still wouldn't budge. The almost neck-high water was lifting him. Afloat, he was losing floor traction. So he braced his back against the doorjamb and started to push instead. He felt movement.

"*Great . . . mother of Russia!*" he howled through gritted teeth.

Slowly, the door slid open, just a crack. When it did,

female fingers poked through the gap above the water line. Then he heard Alex.

"Pull on three!" she called.

And on three, the door shot open.

Hooting in triumph, Chekov rode the escaping wall of water down the corridor. It knocked down Alex and a couple other cadets too. They slid to a stop in front of the elevator doors.

The doors opened. A trio of SFFD firemen stepped out into inches-deep water flowing down the hall. Alex grinned up at them.

"Hi, guys," she said. "Wow, *just in time*."

One of the firemen helped her up. "Glad we could help," he said with an ironic smile. He watched water pour into the open elevator.

Chekov looked up, then asked, "Can you turn off my room?"

Suddenly Alex's roommate, Salla zh'Tran, burst from their room, then ran into Chekov's. The sprinklers were still spouting water. Salla, an Andorian zhen—the closest to a human female of the four Andorian genders—immediately went to Chekov's workdesk. She wiped off water with a sweep of her blue hand.

"Give me a spoon, Pavel," she ordered.

Chekov and Alex stepped inside. "What?"

"A spoon! Or any utensil, please." Salla tossed her

head. A spray of water flew in a ring from her snow-white hair.

Chekov handed her his Red Army knife. Salla quickly pried up the desk's wrist bar. Then she pushed a small red button underneath.

The sprinkler system shut down. The screen went black. All was quiet.

Chekov was dumbfounded.

"What did you do?" he asked.

Salla unleashed her blue smile on him. "Local network kill switch," she said.

"We have *kill* switches?" said Chekov. "They never told me that."

"No, Pavel, they did not," said Salla. "I had to find it myself, in my own desk. Just now."

Chekov stared at her. All at once he found her eerily, painfully beautiful. She was soaking wet. Her Academy uniform clung like a second skin. Even her cranial antennae looked sexy. And she was brilliant.

It was almost too much.

Alex Leigh squeezed water from her dark ponytail, then threw her arm around Salla's neck. "You rock, roomie." She smiled at Chekov.

"Got any towels, kid?" she asked.

• · ·✦· · ✦ · ✦ ·· ·

Meanwhile, Kirk kept spilling things.

He dropped black bean sauce on his lap. A garlic shrimp flipped out of his chopsticks, then bounced across the workdesk. When he reached for a napkin, he knocked over the fried rice.

"You should put food in your *mouth*," suggested T'Laya in a teasing voice. "Really, it tastes better that way."

Kirk looked up at the ceiling.

"Apparently, this infection has destroyed my fine motor skills," he said.

T'Laya closed up a food carton. "What do you need *those* for?"

Kirk gave her a look. He was still trying to figure out when she was kidding and when she was serious. She had a hell of a sense of humor.

"Racquetball," he said.

T'Laya brightened. "You play racquetball?"

"No," said Kirk.

The two cadets had been eating and swapping stories. Back at Medical, he'd learned from McCoy how T'Laya and Uhura had broken up their fight with the upperclassmen. Now she frankly admitted to being fascinated by Kirk's growing legend in their class.

Kirk was disbelieving. "Come on," he said.

"No, I keep hearing things about you," she insisted.

"Like what?"

"Like, how jealous most people are of you," said T'Laya. "That's my take, anyway."

Kirk laughed. "Jealous of me? I can't even use chopsticks," he said, waving them awkwardly in front of him.

"And some of the Command College people think you cheat," she said quietly.

Kirk's smile faded quickly.

He said, "You're kidding, right?"

"I'm not." She leaned back on the bed. "I mean . . . let's face it, you're the only one who beats Viktor Tikhonov regularly."

Kirk looked puzzled. "So?"

T'Laya just looked at him, then shrugged.

"Hey, I beat him in the simulators," said Kirk, irritated. "But he's beat me a few times. Viktor beats everyone else, always. Do they think *he* cheats?"

"Like I said, it's jealousy," replied T'Laya.

"Why aren't they suspicious of Tikhonov?" complained Kirk.

"Because he's not you. He's intense," she said. "He's scary. He's relentless. He makes opponents feel like they're *supposed* to lose." She pointed at Kirk. "But you kick everyone's ass and look like you're not even trying."

Kirk was agitated now. "Maybe because I spend half my waking hours in the Command simulators," he said.

"Do you?" asked T'Laya.

"Do you think I'm *lying*?"

"No," she said. She looked thoughtful. "But why *do* you? Are you afraid of failure?"

Kirk was annoyed now. "Are you joking?"

T'Laya held up her hands. "Easy there, big boy. Don't shoot the messenger."

It was true: Kirk hated to lose. But the other truth was that he *never* thought about failure. It just wasn't on his list of options, so fear of failure wasn't a motivation. There was a more essential reason why he spent so much time in the Command College training environment labs.

"I love the simulators," he said. "That's why."

"You *love* them?"

"Yes," said Kirk.

T'Laya was indeed fascinated. "What do you mean by that?" she asked.

"Surely you can extrapolate my meaning," said Kirk, still a little irritated. "Don't *you* love anything?"

T'Laya looked a little defensive. "Of course I do," she said. "There are things I'm *very* passionate about."

"Like what?" asked Kirk.

"Maybe I'll tell you someday," she replied. "When I get to know you better." She was aiming for flirtatious, but Kirk was too distracted to notice. He stood up, pacing.

"People think I *cheat*?" he muttered.

T'Laya observed his distress and searched for the

right thing to say. "If it makes you feel any better, everyone always wants to be on your team," she said after a moment.

Kirk looked over at her. "Now *you're* lying."

"No, I'm not," she said. "Apparently, you're a born captain. People may be jealous of your success, but they desire your leadership." She rolled over onto her side and propped her head up on her hand. "Let's analyze why, shall we?"

Kirk stopped pacing. "I'm starting to feel like a research project."

T'Laya smiled, happy to see that some of the tension had drained from his face. "I have theories, Kirk," she said.

"I'm sure you do."

"Here's one," she said. "Have you seen that barefoot cadet always running around campus?"

"He's a *cadet*?" said Kirk, surprised. "Wow. I figured he was a faculty member's kid."

"No, that's Pavel Chekov," she said. "He's a brilliant Russian kid who is laying waste to his astrogation and stellar cartography classes."

Kirk nodded. "Ah," he said. "Another growing legend." He was about to make a crack about her being a legend groupie but thought better of it. He sat on the bed. "So . . . what's your theory?"

"I think it's a Tarahumara thing," she said.

"What's that?"

"You've never heard of them?" she asked. When Kirk shook his head no, she went on. "The Tarahumara are a native tribe in the Copper Canyons of northern Mexico. They're incredible athletes. They can run through the mountains for literally hundreds of miles nonstop. And they do it barefoot. You know, all of you Humans evolved from running forebears. And those ancestors . . . they ran barefoot. Your species was shaped by genetics to run great distances—your feet are marvels of evolution. The Human foot is the perfect load-bearing locomotive mechanism."

Kirk shook his head. "I'm not following your famous Vulcan logic here," he said.

"Bear with me," she said.

Kirk leaned a bit closer. "I'll try," he said. "But I'm a little distracted."

T'Laya tossed a pillow at him. Kirk caught it deftly.

"Nice motor skills," she said with a sly smile.

"You have no idea," he said. "But finish your theory,"

"Okay," she said, looking momentarily distracted herself. "So . . . sociologists and evolutionary biologists and college track coaches studied the Tarahumara tribe for years. . . . You know, looking for their *secret*, the thing that makes them such great runners. Were they born with some special quality, some genetic quirk that nobody else had? Turns out, not really, although running barefoot gave them an edge. It kept the Tarahumara in touch with these ancient, powerful physical tools that most Humans have left behind."

Kirk leaned back on his elbows. Her voice was almost hypnotic.

"So what was it?" he asked.

"Love," she said.

Kirk smiled. "Love?"

"That's it. Love."

Kirk nodded, thinking. "They love to run," he said.

"Exactly!"

T'Laya was very animated now. Kirk suspected that this topic was one of her passions. She sat up now, clutching Kirk's other pillow to her chest.

"The Tarahumara once sent a team of their best runners to an ultramarathon in Colorado," she said. "A day-long, hundred-mile race on mountain trails above ten thousand feet. Runners consider it a lonely, grueling endurance test. Some runners barely survive it. But observers along the route noticed something crazy about the Tarahumara team. First they ran together much of the race, flowing along the trails in their bright, ceremonial robes. Second they passed every checkpoint smiling, chatting, and even laughing as they ran. Most other runners ran alone . . . grim islands of pain, pushing along in stoic silence. For the Tarahumara the entire experience was like a day in the park. It wasn't a test of will, nor was it a proving ground. It was just a thing that they love to do."

Kirk reached carefully to touch her hand. She let him grasp her fingers.

"That's *your* secret," she said. "A great starship captain loves his crew, loves his ship, and loves every aspect of his mission." She looked into Kirk's eyes. "That's my theory, anyway."

"I like it," said Kirk.

"So the question becomes, how does passion develop?" she continued. "Is it the product of a unique childhood? Is it a random accident of personality or neurology? Or is it something you can replicate? What if we could train future starship commanders to be like you, Kirk?"

Kirk grinned. "Then Starfleet would be a barking madhouse full of loose cannons."

Now T'Laya's face moved toward his. She put her hand lightly on his neck.

And once again: a loud knock on the door.

"I believe I'm going to ignore that," said Kirk, sliding his arms around T'Laya.

But T'Laya looked uncomfortable as the knocking insistently continued.

"Sounds like business," she said, pulling away reluctantly.

Kirk rolled his eyes.

"Unbelievable," he said.

He got up to activate the door. It slid open to reveal a beautiful woman in a black Starfleet jumpsuit. Her eyes were like blue neon.

"Mr. Kirk," she said with a nod.

Kirk pointed. "I know you," he said.

"I'm surprised that you remember," she replied. "I'm Lieutenant Caan, Starfleet Intelligence. And this is Ensign Collins, Security."

Kirk glanced past her at a stout man wearing a red Starfleet Security uniform. He nodded at Kirk. Kirk nodded back.

"Am I under arrest?" he asked with a smile.

"Not exactly," said Lieutenant Caan.

Now Kirk frowned. "What does that mean?"

"You have orders to appear in the Commandant of Midshipmen's office at 1300 hours." She glanced at her watch. "That would be in seven minutes." Her eyes darted past Kirk to Cadet T'Laya, who still sat on the bed, as she added: "I've been ordered to provide you with a security escort."

"Gosh, Lieutenant," said Kirk. "That's sweet of you."

Lieutenant Caan looked him over. With the shadow of a smile, she said, "Since you're fully uniformed, Mr. Kirk, I suggest we leave immediately."

Kirk nodded. "Sure," he said. "Say, I don't suppose you know what this is about?"

"Actually, I do," said Lieutenant Caan. "I was informed that you've been charged with fifteen separate violations of the Cadet Honor Code."

Kirk turned his head a bit, narrowing his eyes at her.

He said, "This is a mistake."

"For your sake, I hope so, Mr. Kirk," said Lieutenant Caan. "Code violations apply only to your Academy status. I'd be more concerned about the two alleged offenses that fall under jurisdiction of the Punitive Articles of the Uniform Code of Military Justice. As a Starfleet cadet, you're considered military personnel and may be required to face a court-martial proceeding."

Now Kirk's face morphed to disbelief.

"What?" he said. "This . . . this is *not* right."

T'Laya rose from the bed and quickly moved beside Kirk.

"Don't say anything more," she said quietly. "Not until you can meet a JAG." JAG was the acronym for Judge Advocate General, a military lawyer familiar with Starfleet legal code.

Lieutenant Caan turned to her, nodding.

"Good advice, Cadet," said Lieutenant Caan. Then she turned back to Kirk. "If this issue continues beyond the meeting we are about to attend with the commandant, you will be assigned counsel. For now, I'm required by UMCJ Article Thirty-One to inform you that coercive self-incrimination is prohibited. You do indeed have the right to remain silent."

Kirk strode past her to Ensign Collins in the hall.

"You don't have to cuff me, do you?" he asked.

Collins shook his head.

"Are you fast?" asked Kirk.

Collins said, "Very fast." He held up a phaser. "And I'm armed."

"Okay." Kirk nodded. "I'll go quietly."

Collins grinned. "We can talk about the Giants, if you want."

"Nah," said Kirk. "The way they're hitting right now, I'd only get depressed."

As Kirk and Ensign Collins headed down the corridor, T'Laya and Lieutenant Caan exchanged a glance.

"Are you a friend, Cadet?" asked Lieutenant Caan.

"We just met," said T'Laya. "But the answer is yes."

"Let's hope he's innocent," said Lieutenant Caan with a thin smile as she turned to go.

"Mr. Kirk may not be guilty of these particular charges," said T'Laya, returning the smile. "But innocent? Not a chance."

CH.8.13
Code of Conduct

The first time Spock hit a racquetball, it splintered into jagged chunks of blue rubber. Uhura had to crouch and cover as the shards ricocheted around the court. Spock watched the pieces bounce.

"Do I get points for that?" he asked.

"You do in *my* book," said Uhura with a grin.

"What book is that?" asked Spock.

Uhura laughed. Spock just looked at her, waiting for more.

"Never mind," she said.

"I assume that was a defective ball," said Spock as he started to pick up pieces.

"I don't think so, Commander," said Uhura. "I forgot about Vulcan strength. You'll just have to swing a little easier."

She stepped outside the court to pluck a new ball from her sports duffel. As she did so, she sneaked a peek at Spock as he crouched to pick up chunks of rubber. He was fit, but didn't look particularly "athletic" in the Human sense. But Uhura knew all about Vulcan physiology, thanks to some database research that she hoped Spock would never find out she'd conducted. She knew homeworld-raised Vulcans were roughly three times stronger than Humans. She knew they rigorously practiced various forms of martial arts. And she knew they were fully Humanoid in every important physical aspect.

As Uhura stepped back into the court, Spock was closely examining the rubber pieces.

"Can you fix it?" joked Uhura.

"On Vulcan, we synthesize a carbolitic polymer that exhibits superior isotropic hyper-elasticity," he said. He looked at her with an ironic gleam in his eye. "I believe it would make a better ball."

"Would it be Vulcan-proof?" she asked.

"Nothing is Vulcan-proof," he replied.

Her eyes lit up. "We'll just *see* about that," she said. "My serve."

They proceeded to whack the ball around for a solid, sweaty hour. Uhura was a fluid athlete and had played competitive racquetball in school, so she enjoyed a teacher-student role reversal. Spock mastered the court geometry quickly, figuring out shot angles. His superb agility was surprising too. And of course his swing was powerful. But Uhura's deft touch was unbeatable.

"That's match," she called as Spock lunged and missed yet another of her crafty low lobs that dinked off the front wall.

Spock, who had spoken little during the match, picked up the ball and handed it to Uhura.

"You are quite good," he said, smiling.

Uhura hadn't seen a full smile from Spock in weeks. She felt a little weak in the knees.

"Thank you," she replied.

They sat on a bench outside the court. Uhura handed Spock a towel and a hydro-protein drink, then packed their racquets into her duffel. The indoor racquetball courts were part of the Academy's Sports Complex. Many cadets were using the facility that day. With finals and Zeta assignments coming up, a lot of stress hormones needed metabolizing.

"I met someone interesting in the Romulan Archives the other day," said Uhura casually.

Spock drank thirstily. Then he carefully wiped his mouth and said, "How so?"

"Do you remember the girl at the next station?" she asked.

Spock arched an eyebrow, thinking. Then he shook his head.

Uhura said, "She was Vulcan."

"Really?" said Spock. "I did not notice her."

Good, thought Uhura. But she held out her right arm and said, "She was right next to me."

Spock shook his head again. "I was not at your station long enough," he said apologetically.

Uhura smiled. She couldn't help it.

"Well, this girl—her name is T'Laya—she's full-blooded Vulcan," said Uhura. "But she grew up on other planets, including here, on Earth. In fact, she sounded more like an Earth girl than . . . well, than *I* do."

"Vulcans, like Humans, are quite adaptable, both physically and culturally," said Spock.

"I found it interesting," said Uhura.

"Would you like some lunch?" asked Spock suddenly.

"Uh, sure," said Uhura.

"I discovered some anomalous fricatives in the Romulan phonology database we are building from the Cheron recordings," he said. He stood up. "I would like to discuss them with you. Have you ever been to the faculty dining hall?"

Uhura raised her eyebrows.

"No!" she said. "That's an honor for which I feel . . . unworthy."

Spock smiled again. *That's two smiles,* counted Uhura. *He's almost giddy today.*

"I assure you, it is no great honor to eat there, as the

food is rather ordinary," said Spock. "But if it were, you would be more than worthy."

Now Uhura smiled.

"I'm starving," she said.

"As I said, the food is not gourmet, but the top-floor view of the bay and the city skyline is quite striking."

As they strolled across campus, Uhura noticed a few male cadets eyeing her. Then she remembered that she'd hiked up her racquet skirt a bit higher than usual for today's match. She discreetly unrolled the waistband and tugged the skirt lower.

"Commander, I'm going to ask you something that may not be entirely ethical," she said.

Spock raised an eyebrow. "Really?"

"Yes," said Uhura.

"Will it violate the Code of Conduct?" asked Spock.

"I don't think so," replied Uhura. "But I have to ask anyway."

"Well," said Spock. "If you must."

She leaned in closer and lowered her voice. "You have input into the Zeta starship assignments, correct?"

Spock nodded gravely.

Uhura started to speak again, then felt a wave of guilt.

"Never mind," she said, pulling back. "I'm sorry."

Spock stopped walking, turning to her.

"Cadet," he said. "Are you asking me to exert influence

in your favor for a particular ship assignment?"

"No!" replied Uhura, aghast.

Spock just looked at her. They stood now in the entry courtyard of the main building, site of most Academy administrative facilities, including the commandant's suite and the faculty dining hall.

Distressed now, Uhura began, "Commander, I—"

"Nyota, listen to me," he said firmly.

Uhura literally froze. It was the first time he had ever used her given name.

"The faculty senate has appointed me the primary starship assignor," said Spock. "I am in charge of the posting committee. My decisions on personnel assignments for the Zeta exercise are final." With a puzzled look he added, "Nobody is *supposed* to know this. Yet somehow, everybody *does*."

"Well, *I* didn't know," protested Uhura.

Spock raised his hands.

"I believe you, of course," he said. "And in any case, acquiring knowledge, no matter how, is rarely a dishonorable thing, Cadet. Human networks of interpersonal communication are just so remarkably well attuned. It is *fascinating*." He shook his head. "One of my colleagues calls it 'the grapevine.' An apt metaphor, I must say."

"Yeah, word gets around," said Uhura, still looking a bit uneasy.

Spock gently touched her arm. Then he nodded toward a dozen first-year cadets hanging out on the wide staircase leading up to the main building entrance.

"See that group?" he said. "Four of those cadets have approached me in the past week about Zeta assignments." He looked at her. "The ambitious ones."

"The obsequious brownnosers," said Uhura.

"The ambitious ones," corrected Spock.

He led Uhura to a bench, and they both sat. Then he gazed up at the towering statue in the center of the courtyard: Admiral David Glasgow Farragut, the famous Civil War Naval flag officer who became the first Rear Admiral in United States history.

"The USS *Farragut*," he said. "You wish to serve onboard."

Uhura didn't speak.

"It is not code violation to lobby for what you want, Cadet," said Spock. "Let me tell you something important about Starfleet. It is like any other organization in the galaxy. Decisions and appointments have a political component, and sometimes a personal component. Putting together a ship's roster must take many things into account. After all, a starship crew is like a sports team. Raw skill is important. But interpersonal dynamics are critical. I believe your term for it is . . . 'good chemistry.'"

Uhura took a deep breath.

"I wasn't going to ask for a favor, Commander," she said. "I just wanted to know if the rosters were final yet. But yes . . . I did want some insight on how to influence the selection committee."

Spock couldn't hide his amusement.

"I believe the selection committee has already been *deeply* influenced," he said. "And the rosters are final for Friday's posting. I seem to recall that you have been assigned to the communications desk on the bridge of the *Farragut*."

Uhura fought back a wave of emotion.

Then she said, "Thank you, Commander."

Spock stood abruptly.

"I know you were not asking me for favors," he said. "But now I am asking you for one."

Uhura stood too. "Yes?"

"When we are not in uniform," he began, and then hesitated, thinking of how to best phrase his request. "I would prefer that you call me 'Spock' instead of 'Commander.' Of course, it *is* quite rare that we are out of uniform, you and I. We seem to be wedded to our Starfleet tasks. But . . ."

"Spock," said Uhura. She smiled.

Spock smiled back.

"Thank you, Cadet," he said.

"That would be *Nyota* to you," she said. "Maybe you haven't noticed that we're currently out of uniform?"

Spock's eyes flitted down to her skirt and then back.

"Oh, I have noticed," he said.

Lieutenant Commander Judy Renfield, adjutant to the Commandant of Midshipmen, was a frightening woman and a walking rulebook. She was forty-six but dressed and acted older. She pulled her prematurely gray hair into a severe bun. She despised infractions. In fact, whenever she had to say the word, she whispered it as if it suggested something too depraved to speak aloud.

But oddly, in spite of all of this, she liked Kirk.

"I usually enjoy our little visits," said Renfield to Kirk as he sat near her desk in the Commandant's waiting room. "Perhaps they're a little too *frequent*. But they're always fun."

"Agreed," said Kirk.

Renfield gave him a sharp look. "This time . . . not so fun," she said.

Kirk waggled his eyebrows.

"But, Judy," he said. "I found a new, *very* obscure primary source on Admiral Yamamoto's dispersal strategy at Midway."

On one of Kirk's many visits, he and Renfield learned they shared a fascination with the 1942 Battle of Midway, the tide-turning WWII naval engagement between the

United States and Japan in the Pacific. Military historians still considered it the most stunning and decisive blow in the history of naval warfare.

But Renfield shook her head.

"Maybe we can talk about it when you get out of prison in ten years," she said. "Assuming, of course, you're not executed."

Kirk nodded, but he stood to grab a pen from Renfield's desk. Then he jotted something on her sticky notepad.

"Here's the Library of Congress number," he said. "You won't find it online. You'll have to file a request with the LOC war archives division."

A grim Renfield watched with disapproval as Kirk wrote. But when he sat back down, she quickly nabbed the sticky note, slipping it into her pocket.

Kirk noticed but grinned without looking at her.

Something on Renfield's desktop dinged softly, like a bell. She tapped her screen, then looked at Kirk, nodding. Without speaking she pointed over her shoulder at the commandant's office door.

"And here we go," said Kirk, standing.

Ensign Collins, who sat nearby, stood too. But the lieutenant commander held up one finger, then looked at him. Collins smiled and sat back down.

Kirk sighed and entered Vice Admiral Tullsey's office alone.

He found the admiral scribbling furiously on a notepad next to what looked like a dossier.

In a chair beside Tullsey's desk sat Lieutenant Caan. She looked up as Kirk entered, and they made brief eye contact. Once again Kirk found her eyes mesmerizing. Their impossible bright blue glimmer seemed beyond Human, and now he noticed an exotic, alien curve to her face.

"Sit down, Mr. Kirk," said the commandant with a brusque jab toward an empty chair.

"Admiral, I'd really like to—," began Kirk, but Tullsey cut him off sharply.

"Cadet, I strongly advise you to speak as little as possible until you know what's going on," he rumbled.

"Yes, sir," said Kirk with a quick nod. He sat.

Admiral Tullsey muttered to himself for a while longer, shaking his head as he flipped through a few more pages of the dossier. He jotted more notes. His old-fashioned reading glasses gave him a professorial look, but Kirk knew better. The vice admiral was a bulldog with both bark *and* bite. Finally he flipped the report shut and then gave it a resolute slap.

"Mr. Kirk, I find this entirely . . . unbelievable," he said.

"As do I, sir," said Kirk.

"Do you *know* what's in here?" said the admiral, tapping the dossier.

"No, sir."

Kirk glanced over at Lieutenant Caan, who was staring directly into his eyes. Her demeanor was calm and watchful. Kirk held her gaze for a few seconds: Her eyes widened slightly as he did. A hint of a smile rippled across her pale lips.

"This may seem trite or quaint, Mr. Kirk, but I'd like you to recite the Cadet Honor Code if you would," said the admiral.

This was not an unreasonable request. The Honor Code was a single sentence. First-year cadets were often ordered to repeat it, frequently by upperclassmen in the first weeks of term, and Kirk knew it well.

He said, "A cadet will not lie, cheat, steal, or tolerate those who do."

"Thank you," said the admiral. He patted the dossier on his desk. "I'm going to let you read this entire sordid report in a minute, but let me give you a summary." He glanced down at his notes. "Violations of the Honor Code include cheating, plagiarism, lying to achieve unfair advantage, and theft. Add to that numerous regulatory infractions, including multiple curfew and residence hall violations; unauthorized female visitors after-hours, both cadet and civilian; and, uh, other activities . . . drunk and disorderly activity.

Good god, I could go on for a while, but I won't."

Tullsey glared at Kirk over the top of his reading glasses.

Kirk considered his words carefully.

Then he said, "Admiral, I have never committed an Honor Code violation." He looked at Lieutenant Caan. "Never."

Tullsey nodded. He said, "And these regulatory infractions?"

Kirk hesitated. Then he said, "Maybe a few of them . . . ?"

Tullsey almost smiled but caught himself.

"Okay, well . . . we'll deal with these accusations individually in a moment," he said. "But the lieutenant here has evidence of a much more serious offense, one that could be considered criminal in nature, and which certainly violates the Uniform Code of Military Justice." He looked at Lieutenant Caan.

"Actually, it's two offenses," said Lieutenant Caan in a measured tone. "We have evidence suggesting that you, Cadet Kirk, may have tampered with Starfleet internal operating systems in a malicious manner. It also appears that you targeted a fellow cadet with this activity . . . and that the alleged activity threatened the life of that cadet. You should also know that Starfleet Intelligence is now investigating a large number of unauthorized and possibly illegal database searches originating from your secure Starfleet account."

Kirk was stunned silent for a moment. He turned to Admiral Tullsey, who looked uncomfortable.

Finally, Kirk said, "Admiral?"

Tullsey cleared his throat. Then he drew a deep breath and said, "Mr. Kirk, I don't like Intelligence snooping around in Academy matters. I've made that perfectly clear to Lieutenant Caan, here. We take care of our own, as a general rule." He leaned his arms heavily on the desk, then leveled his eyes at Kirk's. "But the incident she refers to happened today in Nimitz Hall, and it did indeed target a cadet, a first-year. And, son . . . it was clearly malicious in nature, and could've had deadly consequences."

Kirk looked at Lieutenant Caan. Something about her manner of presentation seemed odd. Then it hit him.

"Wait. You don't think I did it, do you?" he asked.

Lieutenant Caan was taken aback. She said, "We grant you the presumption of innocence."

Kirk laughed. With an involuntary edge of sarcasm, he said, "Right. Starfleet Intelligence is really known for its restraint."

Lieutenant Caan turned to the admiral.

"May I speak freely and . . . confidentially, sir?" she asked.

"Absolutely!" barked Tullsey. "This room is secure."

Kirk gave Lieutenant Caan a dark look. "I wouldn't count on that, sir."

Her tone grew chilly in response. "Mr. Kirk, you disappeared two nights ago for a period of six hours," she said.

"It seems so," he replied.

"Yes, it does," she said. "And you claim to have no recollection of your activities during that period, correct?"

"It's not a *claim*," he said. "It's a fact."

Lieutenant Caan reached into a uniform pouch, producing a digital notepad. She tapped it a few times, then stood to hand the display to Kirk.

"What's this?" asked Kirk, taking it.

"These are Dr. McCoy's diagnostic notes and other observations related to your hospitalization," she said. "I've come to respect Dr. McCoy's insight into your case. He seems like a man of integrity, and he's very loyal to you."

Kirk smiled slightly as he examined the screen. Then he handed it back.

"You won't find a better man," he said.

Lieutenant Caan remained standing. She was a tall, lithe woman with the figure of a dancer. Her movements were very ballet-precise. She brushed her finger lightly up the notepad several times, scrolling.

"Now, Mr. Kirk, keep in mind that you do have the right to remain silent, so I want you to answer carefully," she said. "I want to protect you. But I'm going to ask you a couple of admittedly odd-sounding questions."

Kirk was wary. She seemed sincere. And on another level, he liked her—the voice and movement and eyes, those neon eyes. But nobody trusted the black jumpsuit of Starfleet Intelligence, no matter how good it looked on her.

"Okay, shoot," said Kirk finally.

Lieutenant Caan looked at her screen. Then she looked at Kirk and asked, "Are you a quarry rat?"

Kirk twitched in surprise. Then he frowned.

"Hell yes, I'm a quarry rat," he said.

Lieutenant Caan nodded. She said, "Dr. McCoy's notes mention that you reported flashbacks, a flood of boyhood memories, a *strong* flood, washing over you since your episode. Can you describe these to me?"

Kirk's eyes narrowed. "Why?" he asked.

"Are Dr. McCoy's notes correct?" she responded.

Kirk nodded. "Yes," he said.

"Do the flashbacks include memories of swimming in the dark water of a quarry? Make that cold and dark waters?"

"Yes," said Kirk.

"This quarry is in Iowa, correct?" asked Lieutenant Caan.

"I grew up near the Riverside Shipyards. But of course you already knew that."

"I did," said Lieutenant Caan. "I know about the local

rock quarry. And about your brother, George Samuel Kirk. He's in your flashbacks too, right?"

Kirk nodded again. "Yes, I told Bones about those images. Very vivid. Very . . . present." He leaned back in his chair. "Lieutenant, why is this important to the question of these charges?"

Lieutenant Caan sat back down and then examined her notepad again.

"The cadet victim of the incident at Nimitz Hall reported that an image appeared on his workdesk viewscreen during the incident in question," she said. "Our cyber-crime people managed to recover the image. It was deliberately distorted, but here it is."

She tapped on the screen and then handed the display to Kirk.

"Just tap the play icon," she said.

Kirk did so and then watched the recording. Then he lowered the pad to his lap.

"My god," he said.

"Mr. Kirk," said Lieutenant Caan slowly. "Would you say this recording conveys certain information that only *you* would know?"

Kirk knew that his answer would be self-incriminating. But he was ready to answer . . . when suddenly Admiral Tullsey interrupted.

"I'm sure Cadet Kirk wants the whole truth to come

out," said the admiral. "But, Cadet, I would suggest that you don't answer that question. Not yet, anyway."

Lieutenant Caan nodded. "Actually, I agree," she said to Tullsey. Then she pointed at the dossier. "Doesn't it seem odd to you, Admiral, that all of these incident reports came flowing in at once?"

"The timing is quite curious," said the admiral.

"And all of them are anonymous reports?" she asked.

"Every one," said Admiral Tullsey. "Except for tonight's incident in Nimitz, of course."

Kirk glanced down at the notepad display in his hands. Up in the corner, text in a tiny font read: CHEKOV, PAVEL. NIMITZ 316. FIRST-YEAR. He handed the notepad back to the lieutenant.

Then Kirk dropped his aching head into his hands.

I need help, he thought.

But he wasn't exactly sure what kind.

Uhura swept her gaze across the horizon.

Spock was right: The view from the dining hall was astounding. It was a perfect afternoon—azure sky, cerulean water, riffled by a landward breeze. Sailboat spinnakers dotted the bay.

"How is your minestrone?" asked Spock.

"Good," said Uhura. "And your plomeek broth?"

"It is very good," he said.

"Isn't that traditionally a morning meal on Vulcan?" she asked.

Spock was impressed. "Yes, commonly," he said. "But it is the only native Vulcan dish that I find edible in this dining hall."

Uhura grinned. She sipped her water . . . then tried to sound casual.

"My comparative exobiology professor said something interesting today," she said. "Biological similarities between most known Humanoid species in our galaxy suggest that our origins may *all* trace back to a single seed genetic code."

Spock nodded. "An entirely logical assumption," he said.

"The theory is that a space-faring, warp-capable civilization preceded us, perhaps by millions of years . . . then disappeared," she said. "That's mind-blowing."

"Certainly, my own existence suggests a common Vulcan-Human ancestry," replied Spock. "My father's Vulcan sperm found my mother's Human egg to be a hospitable destination, genetically speaking, and thus here I am."

Gosh, how romantic, thought Uhura.

"Why did they marry?" she asked.

Spock looked slightly startled.

Uhura put her hand on the table. "I'm sorry if that's too

forward. I know it's a pretty personal question."

"That is okay," replied Spock. "I admire Humans who get right to the point. Most do not."

"Well, *I* do," said Uhura.

"Yes," agreed Spock. "My father was Vulcan's ambassador to Earth for many years. That is how he met my mother. He once told me that, given his position, marrying an Earth Human was the logical thing to do."

"Touching," said Uhura.

Spock was amused. "However, I do believe he has *feelings* for her," he said. "As do I."

Uhura nodded. *Time to change the subject,* she thought. "It's a little unsettling to think that Romulans might share our genetic roots too," she said.

"Why?" asked Spock.

Uhura thought for a moment, then said, "I guess because I grew up afraid of Romulans. They were the great evil, unknown and unseen, like monsters lurking out there beyond the Neutral Zone."

Spock took a sip of his plomeek broth while he considered this.

"On Earth your French and English subcultures fought many bloody wars over the centuries," he said. "By your logic they should find their common DNA most unsettling to contemplate."

"I think they do," replied Uhura, laughing.

"I will consult with Professor Galloway on that," said Spock, amused.

"But I get your point," said Uhura. "See, for Humans, Romulans are like phantoms." She curled her fingers like claws, waving her hands. "They're the *bogeymen*. If we had any kind of direct cultural contact, maybe that perception would change."

"For Vulcans the Romulan genetic connection is likely, and recent," said Spock. "Many Vulcan scholars believe that today's Romulan race traces its roots to a group of Vulcan separatists who fled our planet more than two millennia ago."

Uhura almost dropped her soupspoon.

"Romulans are direct descendants of Vulcans?" she asked.

Spock nodded. "Most likely, although this has never been verified."

"Why did these separatists leave Vulcan?"

"The reasons are complex," said Spock. "But in essence, they left to escape the Great Awakening, our cultural movement that established the purging of emotions in favor of logic."

Uhura lifted her shoulders.

"Wow, Romulan cousins," she said. "That could complicate things at holiday reunions."

Spock smiled, then looked out the window. "As you

know, we fought a terrible hundred-year war with the Star Empire not so long ago, beginning in the middle of your twentieth century," he said. "Yet despite that fact, a few radical factions on our planet consider the Vulcan-Romulan kinship link to be significant. In fact, they believe a racial reunification is not only desirable, but inevitable."

"There are Vulcans who are Romulan *sympathizers?*" asked Uhura.

"They are rare," said Spock. "But they do exist."

Uhura's communicator beeped. She pulled it from her waist-pouch and then looked. It was a message from Leonard McCoy.

It read: *Jim needs help. Meet us at Medical ASAP.*

She looked at Spock.

He nodded. "It would appear that you need to go," he said, noting her concerned expression.

She looked at the message again. Then a second message from McCoy appeared.

This one read: *Doesn't look good.*

CH.9.13
All Hands on Deck

Nverinn knew his agent would be aggressive.

She was designed to be. The AI parameters allowed her great freedom in pursuing objectives. Thus it wasn't entirely inconceivable that in carrying out a simple decoy operation, Gemini nearly killed a kid.

But Nverinn was furious nonetheless.

"This is precisely the kind of mistake I warned about," he said into his desk mike. He spoke in flat, unemotional tones—in Nverinn's case, a sure sign of anger. "It could attract attention."

"It already has," said the agent.

"How so?"

"Starfleet Intelligence is very involved."

Nverinn wanted to pound the desk. But he would never do that.

"Gemini," he said, "building the database is what's mission critical. *That's* your focus, not this other stuff. The disruption activity is secondary to your primary mission. You must remember that."

"Understood."

Nverinn pinched the ridges above his nose.

"Let's suspend all the other activities for now," he said. "Focus on the cadet . . . What's his name?"

"James Kirk."

"Yes, this Kirk," said Nverinn. "Let's keep mining that source. Keep drilling."

"The first infection was quite successful," said the agent. "But it inflicted damage."

"Debilitating damage?" asked Nverinn.

"I don't believe so." Subspace distortion static crackled in the transmission. "He's quite fit, with remarkable resilience. But I fear a second round could leave him seriously impaired, if not depleted."

"Let's avoid that, if possible," said Nverinn.

"Understood."

The agent's voice, scrambled on both ends (at its Earth origin and at its Romulus reception), was reconstructed as a cold, metallic hiss. Despite knowing the technical reasons why it sounded so, Nverinn still got a chill when he heard it.

He glanced at the transmission timer.

"We must be quick," he said. "Upload packets now."

The agent's "voice" turned into a babble of upload-

ing code. The data transmission bounced in rapid microbursts between numerous subspace band frequencies to
avoid detection. In theory the microbursts would regis-
ter only as random, acceptable patterns of "chatter" or
spatial anomalies by Federation subspace monitoring
stations. The upload also plotted constantly changing
transmission routes through the Federation's web of subspace relay beacons. But all packets ended up flowing into
the transceiver array that jutted like a titanic spike from the
Center's roof.

Majal approached behind him.

"Is that Gemini?" she asked.

Nverinn spun to face her. She looked anxious. He gave
her a reassuring smile.

"Yes," he said.

"Is everything well?" she asked.

"Gemini is functioning well," Nverinn confirmed with a
nod. "As planned."

The girl sighed. She looked at the incoming telemetry
on Nverinn's display.

"When can I scan the data?" she asked.

Nverinn smiled again. "After you've finished your exercises," he said. "*And* had a snack."

"I don't want a snack," she said. "I will finish my exercises, but there's no reason for me to have a snack if I am
not hungry," she grumbled.

Nverinn understood. A tidal wave of sadness suddenly rolled over him. In that moment Majal reminded him so much of her sister, back before her sister was fully trained.

"You must be regular with your health and exercises," he said. "Just like Gemini was."

"I know," said the girl. She turned and walked out of the lab.

"Good girl," called Nverinn as she left.

A voice suddenly crackled in the workstation speaker. At first it was indistinct, then the words clarified. It was a recording of the voice of James T. Kirk—the first time Nverinn had heard it. Kirk spoke in English, one of the Human languages that Nverinn knew well, but the infection slurred his words. So Nverinn read the auto-transcription printing on-screen as he listened.

The transcript read: "Nobody knows tactical like me, not at the Academy. But that's not it, that's not why you win. You don't win with a playbook. You win with *people*. Good people. Watch next week, watch my team, I promise you we [indecipherable] rock the house. I promise you that. Yeah. [pause] But in the end, so what? It's just a *war game*, you know."

Nverinn was fascinated. He tapped up the volume.

Kirk continued, now sounding less agitated: "Look, you know this, you know my father saved the lives of eight hundred Starfleet personnel . . . including my own . . . during the twelve minutes he served as captain of a starship. He did it by flying a straight line into the [inaudible] enemy's teeth. That's it. What tactical knowledge did *that* take? Here's what it is: It's putting your people *first*, and yourself *last*. That's what it took. That's what he did. And Pike wants me to top that? How the [indecipherable] do you top that?"

Nverinn had to smile. He liked this young man. He was a great subject, and they would learn a lot from him.

Then he heard Gemini's voice—her actual voice:

"Become a great man yourself, Mr. Kirk. Make the galaxy a less . . . hostile place. Save lives for fifty years, not just twelve minutes."

Hearing Gemini, the sadness washed over him again.

● · · ✦ ·· ✦ · ✦ ·· ·

Dr. McCoy stood at a wall-size whiteboard in one of the Medical College's lecture halls. He tapped a red dry-erase marker on a crude map of the Academy campus that he'd just drawn.

The others—Kirk, Uhura, and T'Laya—sat in front-row desks.

"Here," said McCoy. "This is where we all saw you last, Jim."

He drew a red *A* in the center of the residence hall quadrangle. It marked the site of Alpha Centauri, the student center with various facilities—mail room, housing services, recreation, vending—plus the on-campus pub, the Perihelion.

"Oh, I remember now," said Kirk. "We were all doing laundry."

Uhura gave him a look.

"Joking," said Kirk. "I remember nothing."

"You don't recall showing that poor bartender how to make a Cardassian Sunrise?" asked Uhura. "You went on for, like, twenty minutes."

"No, I don't," said Kirk.

"It's seared into *my* memory," said T'Laya, sitting next to him.

Kirk shrugged. "Okay, so I'm particular about certain drinks," he said.

T'Laya hooked her hand around Kirk's bicep. "You harassed Uhura about her first name," she said.

"Again?" said Kirk.

"She had to stave you off with a trident."

Uhura laughed. When she saw Kirk's look, she said, "Hey, she's kidding. I told you, you were actually a gentle-man."

Kirk turned to T'Laya. She locked her charcoal gray eyes into his.

"You have smoky eyes," he said.

T'Laya gave him a funny look. "What does that mean?"

"It means stop looking at me," he said, lowering his voice. "I'm having trouble breathing."

She raised an eyebrow and smiled a big, suggestive smile.

McCoy cleared his throat. "Can we get back to saving Jim's ass?" he asked.

Kirk frowned. "Bones, I thought you said I wasn't drunk?"

"You weren't," McCoy insisted. "You ordered a drink but never touched it."

The doctor turned back to the whiteboard, then marked a red *B* on the flower garden outside the Academy Shuttle Hangar.

"Here's where Lieutenant Caan found you," he said to Kirk.

Kirk nodded. The two locations were not far apart.

"Yes," said Kirk. "*That* I remember."

"So let's start with the possibility that Jim just wigged out, walked from *A* to *B*, and collapsed for six hours," said McCoy. "Does anybody have a problem with that?"

Kirk raised his hand and said, "I do."

They all looked at him.

"Why?" asked McCoy.

"I saw the video recording from Cadet Chekov's room link," he said. "It was distorted, but it was me. Looked like me, sounded like me, said things only *I* would know." He leaned his elbows on the desk, running his fingers through his hair.

"But you don't remember ever making the recording," said T'Laya.

"No," said Kirk. "The *only* time it could have happened was during that six-hour gap."

Kirk had already told the group about Chekov's "haunted room" ordeal—he learned the details from the admiral's dossier that included Lieutenant Caan's Intelligence briefing on the incident. Kirk did have programming skills, but the cyber-attack's complexity was light-years beyond his ability.

"Clearly, it's a setup," said McCoy. "Jim, what were you like on that video recording? How did you act?"

"Drugged," said Kirk. "I mean, it was me, but I was . . . not right. I sounded goofy."

"I think you're the fall guy, Kirk," agreed Uhura. "Maybe even the target, ultimately."

"But why me?" asked Kirk.

McCoy and Uhura exchanged a glance.

"What?" asked Kirk, noticing.

"Come on, Jim," said McCoy. "Take a wild guess. Why might someone want you out of commission . . . this week, in particular?"

Kirk looked at T'Laya. She shrugged coyly and said, "Hey, I told you so."

Kirk scoffed.

"Come on," he said. "Are you seriously saying that the attack on Chekov was really an attack on me . . . because people are *jealous*?"

"Makes sense," said T'Laya. "Some cadets will do anything to get the Zeta assignment they want."

Uhura avoided eye contact.

"And that includes turning some kid's room into an aquarium?" said Kirk.

"Maybe it was a prank that got out of hand," added T'Laya. "I really like this jealous cadet angle. . . ."

"Prank?" repeated McCoy. "You drug up a guy and then shoot video of him, then use that in a highly sophisticated cyber-crime that has all the Starfleet tech experts baffled. . . . That's more than a prank."

"It's more like a conspiracy," said Uhura.

"I see your point," T'Laya said, nodding. "But what about Viktor Tikhonov?" she suggested. "He hangs out with that bunch of guys, you know . . . people call them the Russian Mafia. I bet a few of them have top-flight hacker skills."

Kirk shook his head.

"No way," said Kirk. "Viktor already *knows* he's at the top of the Zeta list. Believe me. His arrogance allows for no other possibility. He doesn't need some harebrained scheme to knock me down a notch."

"But Chekov is Russian too, right?" said T'Laya. "Maybe he's in on it."

Kirk gave her a look.

"I just don't see that," he said. "Not Viktor."

But what she said had him thinking: *Chekov. Tikhonov. The Russians.* At the very least it was another reason to visit Nimitz Hall. He knew they both lived there. But he said nothing.

McCoy folded his arms. "Jim, I'd really like to see that video. Maybe I can get a read on your condition at the time."

"You'll have to ask Lieutenant Caan," said Kirk. "It's loaded on her notepad."

McCoy crooked up one eyebrow.

"Well, then," he said. "I might do that. This being official business and whatnot."

Kirk gave him a sly look.

"And hey, Bones, the lieutenant told me she respects your integrity and insight," he said. "I tried to set her straight, but she wouldn't listen."

"What a pal you are," said McCoy.

"That woman is spooky," said Kirk.

"How did she find you in that garden?" asked Uhura suddenly.

Kirk shrugged. "I don't know," he said. "She just followed the trail of drool, I guess."

"The spot is pretty secluded," continued Uhura. "I mean . . . why would she look in there?"

McCoy gave a gruff laugh. "Hey, I was looking in *dumpsters*," he said.

"Right," Uhura agreed, nodding. "I guess we looked in some odd places too."

McCoy turned back to the whiteboard. "I say it's time for some old-school detective work," he said. He drew two crossed lines through the map, splitting the campus into four quadrants, then numbered each quadrant one to four. "Pick a number, folks. Let's split up. Ask people in your quadrant if they saw Jim on Tuesday night during that six-hour gap."

"Split up?" said T'Laya. "What if Kirk bolts again?"

Kirk grinned. "Starfleet Intelligence will 'find' me with extreme prejudice."

McCoy checked his watch. "Meet back here in two hours," he said.

As they exited the lecture hall, the women walked ahead, and Kirk pulled up beside McCoy. "Bones," he said quietly. "Lieutenant Spooky told me she'd be at Campus Security until eight this evening. You should stop in during your search to, uh, see that video." He smiled and gave McCoy a clap on the shoulder. "Her first name is Samarra. But I didn't tell you that."

McCoy nodded. "Thanks, buddy."

"One more thing," Kirk murmured. "I don't think she's all Human, do you?"

"Jim, after the marriage I had, I'd rather date a hairless yellow Aaamazzarite than another Human woman," said McCoy. He glanced up ahead at T'Laya, who chatted with Uhura as they stepped through the Medical College entrance. "And anyway, female aliens can be very interesting, don't you agree?"

Kirk grinned, then said, "Yes, they definitely can be."

Sure, Chekov was a nice kid.

Of all the cadets in Starfleet the young Russian was probably the last one you'd want to cyber-attack. Back in his homeland's online community, with its long history of cyber-crime lords and other malicious wizardry, Chekov was a white-knight legend.

Or at least his screen name, translated from Russian as "MisterCleanUp," was.

Chekov's specialty was tracking down online scam artists and crippling their operations with viral counterattacks. He did it out of a sense of justice instilled by his parents; he also found it great fun. It often meant forays into the deadly cyber-web of the Russian crime syndicates, the most ruthless and lethal on Earth. But Chekov was so good that not even the wizard-level hackers employed by

Russian gangs could find him. Nobody had ever connected the dots between the cyber-kid and the flesh-boy.

With this background it wasn't surprising that Chekov was already hunting the infectious agent that had attacked his room.

And now he had a formidable partner.

"What have you got, Salla?" asked Chekov, typing on his laptop touchscreen at the speed of light.

"This piece is a *very* aggressive searchbot," replied Salla, who was also typing with blinding speed. "Wow. Whenever I get a trace, it just . . . melts away." She shook her head. "I've never seen an agent quite so *agile*. It must re-encode its infection many times per second."

They sat side-by-side in a deserted corner of the cadet lunchroom. Both worked on laptop links with dual quantum cores that they'd specially modified. The computing power at that one table could run an entire city transit system.

Or bring one crashing down, if the user was so inclined.

"Amazing," said Chekov, now shaking his head too.

"What?" asked Salla.

Chekov pointed at his screen. "All *my* trace code gets . . . eaten."

Salla leaned over to examine his screen.

"Have you tried any of those new malware-buster tools I gave you?" she asked.

"Not yet," said Chekov.

"Can I try a couple things?" she asked.

"Oh sure," said Chekov, pushing back his chair a bit.

Salla reached over. As her fingers tapped the screen, she slid in closer to Chekov. Her jasminelike smell made him feel a little woozy. He fought the sudden urge to run his fingers through her soft white hair.

What is wrong with me? he thought.

"Okay, kid, I set up a string," she said. "It's automated and ingenious, if I do say so myself."

Chekov took a deep breath and tried to focus.

"What does it do?" he asked.

Salla grinned. "It punches some nice holes in the bad guy's botnet," she said. "That should be a good kick in the groin for now."

Chekov unconsciously pushed his legs closer together.

"It's got a hell of a defensive grid, though," added Salla in admiration. "It fights back hard. It has a *massive* attack vector. I don't think these are Russians or anyone else I've seen before."

Chekov nodded. "I've never seen an infection quite so robust and . . . *alive*," he said.

Salla glanced at her watch.

"I have to go," she said, jumping up. "I'm almost late for Astrosciences." She flipped her notepad shut, then slipped it into her bookpack on the table.

"How is that class going?" asked Chekov, trying not to sound disappointed that she was leaving.

"Great!" said Salla as she slung the pack over her shoulder. "Except for the Japanese dude, Sulu. He's beaten me on every exam so far by a margin of at least two points." She grinned. "I'm gonna get him next week on the final."

"Good luck," said Chekov.

"You think your room is clean and dry yet?" she asked.

Chekov shrugged. "I'll go check now," he replied.

Salla gave Chekov a good-bye pat on the back, then hurried away. "Let's link up again tonight," she called back. "This is fun."

Chekov brightened.

"Aye!" he replied. "Sounds *good*!"

Chekov watched the air she'd just passed through for a few seconds, still at odds with the clear attraction he was feeling toward his neighbor.

When he reached his room in Nimitz, Chekov was surprised to find it already cleaned up and livable. A building services team had suctioned water from the hall too, and radiant panels along the corridor had dried everything. When Chekov's door closed behind him with its customary whoosh, he immediately crouched to check the manual override latch.

"Ha," he muttered with a grin. "Now I'll *always* know where you are."

But seeing the door shut gave him an involuntary shudder. Giving in to impulse, he double-tapped the open button on the panel. This opened the door . . . and locked it in that position.

Maybe just for a while, he thought.

Now Chekov sat at his workdesk. He noted that his system had already been rebooted. He rested his fingers on the touchscreen for a second, and then typed his login password. His home screen popped up immediately. Chekov took a breath and then smiled.

Then the ceiling lights popped . . . and the room went black.

"Ay, mother," cried Chekov.

Now the memory of his attacker's dark, mocking image rose in his vision. In his mind's eye he saw a monster. He remembered the distorted voice: *Cold water is a bad way to die.* He stared at his glowing workdesk screen. It was still working. What would appear?

And then he heard that voice, though undistorted this time, from his open doorway.

"Mr. Chekov," it said.

Chekov twirled to face the voice. A dark figure, backlit by the corridor lights, stood silhouetted in the doorway.

"Who are you?" asked Chekov.

"I'm a quarry rat," said the figure.

Chekov stood up. "Are you here to kill me?" he asked.

"Nah," said the figure. "Unless of course . . . you can't handle Russian vodka."

The figure held up a bottle.

An hour later, Kirk and Chekov sat side-by-side on the floor of Chekov's room, staring at the Russian's laptop screen.

"So you actually *hate* Tikhonov?" asked Kirk for the third time, watching Chekov type.

"Very deeply," replied Chekov.

"Wow," said Kirk. "So he bullies you."

Chekov shrugged. "He bullies everybody."

Kirk nodded. "True," he said. "But I bet it's worse with his countrymen. Especially when they're two-thirds his age but twice as smart."

Chekov grinned. His visitor, well aware of his age, had been kidding about the vodka. Apparently it was a gift for Tikhonov, which Chekov didn't really understand, but he hadn't asked for a fuller explanation because the sight of Kirk had initially made him so nervous. But it seemed more and more like Kirk really was a good guy. Chekov began to relax.

He pointed to the screen. "Here's more stuff on you. The malicious searchbot extracted this from your files, then stashed it in zombie databases." He tapped the screen.

Kirk rubbed his chin. "So you're saying hundreds of innocent servers across the planet are now storing personal information on James Tiberius Kirk?"

"More like millions," said Chekov. "On dozens of planets. The data are chopped up into very tiny bits."

Kirk started laughing. "Good god, that's hilarious," he said.

"Maybe so," said Chekov. "But it appears to have accessed *all* your Starfleet records—psych profiling, background security check, and full medical tricorder scan files. Whoever's behind this infection has mined enough data to almost *recreate* you."

Kirk stared at the screen. "I can't imagine a bigger waste of time and resources."

A new set of images started streaming on-screen. Chekov watched happily and then said, "Ah, look. Cadet Salla's parasite worm continues to bear fruit. Here's more stolen data on you."

Kirk pointed in disbelief. "Hey, that's my senior year at Riverside Central!"

"It says you got kicked off the basketball team," said Chekov, reading off the screen.

"Yep," said Kirk, smiling nostalgically. "Those were great days." He pointed again. "That's the Riverside Quarry."

Chekov shivered involuntarily. "The one with the cold, dark water?"

"Oh yeah," said Kirk. "Fifty-four degrees. And colder

as you go deeper." He closed his eyes, smiling and remembering. "We used to meet the cheer squad down there. I went skinny-dipping in that quarry for the very first time when I was about your age," he began to reminisce. Then he shook his head as if to clear it, bringing himself back to the present day.

"Tomorrow is a big day," he said to Chekov. "The Zeta ship rosters get posted. Then we'll have our first section meetings."

"Right!" said Chekov. "I forgot."

"You *forgot*?"

Chekov smiled. "I've been busy." He made a swimming motion. "Snorkeling in my room."

Kirk glanced at his watch, then stood up.

"Thanks, kid," he said. "I'm really sorry this happened to you. I appreciate your help." He gave Chekov an earnest look, then added, "Seriously . . . I hope we're on the same bridge someday."

Chekov stood as well. "That would be an adventure," he said.

They shook hands.

"Let me know if you find anything else of interest," said Kirk.

"Aye," said Chekov with a nod.

As Kirk turned to go, he saluted and said, "Full throttle, Mr. Chekov."

"Aye, Captain," said Chekov with an amused return salute.

Kirk walked to the elevator and punched the down button. As he stood waiting, he glanced at the bottle of Stolichnaya he was carrying, remembering what he was going to do with it. Originally his plan had been to share a drink with Chekov, but as soon as he met the kid, he remembered his age and realized he wasn't someone he could share a drink with. But it was no matter . . . He knew another Russian who would enjoy the bottle. *And if that Russian drinks too much the night before a big mission, so be it,* Kirk thought with an amused grin.

He rode down just one floor. Then he went to Nimitz 266 and then knocked on the door.

Viktor Tikhonov answered.

"Kirk!" boomed Tikhonov. His voice was a baritone blast. He glanced down, adding, "What's that?"

Kirk held up the Stolichnaya bottle.

"It's a Molotov cocktail," he said.

Tikhonov smiled. "So you've come to sabotage me?"

"No," said Kirk. "I can't beat you, so I've decided to join you."

Tikhonov laughed appreciatively. Kirk handed him the bottle, and the Russian examined it.

"Ah, the Elit!" he said. "This is very good stuff, Mr. Kirk."

Kirk nodded slightly. "Good luck tomorrow, Viktor."

Tikhonov nodded back.

"I have no doubt we'll be jousting again soon, Kirk," he said with a scary smile.

Viktor Tikhonov unscrewed the bottle cap, took a huge feral swallow, and rammed his palm into the door button. Every move he made was infused with undisguised, unabashed arrogance. His accent wasn't as thick as Chekov's, but it did the job. It said, *Yes, I'm Russian, and I'm going to destroy your puny illusions.*

As the door slid shut, Kirk smiled.

Then he headed back to the Medical College, where he was about to learn some very bad news.

CH.10.13
Dark Angel

The sun had already sizzled into the Pacific behind the Golden Gate Bridge. Kirk jogged down the tree-lined promenade that connected the residence quad with the rest of the campus. As he turned toward the Medical College at a walkway intersection, he felt a rush of blood to his head and stopped.

"Whoa!" he said, leaning over.

Not ready to run yet.

As Kirk let the dizziness pass, he caught a glimpse of a thin, shadowy figure gliding through the trees behind him. He turned to it.

"Uhura?" he called, confused.

The figure disappeared.

Kirk watched for a second: no sign of movement. He turned to take a step, then stopped again. Again he bent down. His vision was gyrating. He wondered if he'd actually seen anything.

After a few seconds, he felt a little better. But he walked slowly the rest of the way.

When Kirk entered the Medical College lecture hall, McCoy took one look at him and then hustled up the center stairs.

"You look terrible," said McCoy.

"I'm okay, Bones," said Kirk, holding up his hands. "Really."

"Don't insult me, Jim," said McCoy. "I'm a doctor."

"Yes," said Kirk. "I believe you've mentioned that before."

"You're flushed and unsteady," said McCoy, sliding a medical tricorder from his hip pouch. "Sit!"

As Kirk slumped into the nearest desk chair, T'Laya approached to feel his forehead.

"No fever, at least," she said.

Kirk looked around. "Where's Uhura?" he asked.

"Not here yet," said T'Laya, sitting in the next chair.

"I think I saw her out on the promenade," said Kirk.

"Wow, you're really sweating," said T'Laya. Looking upset, she started rubbing Kirk's back.

Kirk wiped his forehead.

"Well, I ran here," he said. He squinted and looked at T'Laya through one eye. "Sort of."

McCoy was waving the tricorder around Kirk's head and shoulders. "Heart rate elevated," he said. "I don't like this. Your thyroxines are sky-high."

"Oh, I do that on purpose," said Kirk.

"Not funny, Jim," said McCoy. "It means your metabolic rate is going wacko again."

"I just need to rest a minute," said Kirk.

McCoy said, "If this keeps up, you'll be resting in my ICU again."

Kirk gave him a ragged smile. "Only if they give me the *good* ice cream this time," he said. Then he turned to T'Laya.

Her eyes were shimmering wet.

"Whoa there, darlin'. I'm okay. Really." He grabbed her hand. "Hey."

She tried to speak but couldn't. For a few seconds she could only blink out tears.

Kirk put his hand on her cheek. "I thought Vulcans were big on logic and stuff," he said. He flicked away a descending tear with his thumb. "Crying isn't logical."

"I guess I'm a bad Vulcan," she said.

Kirk grinned. "I like my Vulcans bad."

McCoy sat down heavily in the chair on Kirk's other side.

"Listen, Jim, we've got some news," he said. He looked over at T'Laya. "It's not good, and given your condition right now, the timing is terrible. But the sooner you know, the better."

Kirk saw that McCoy was grimly serious. And T'Laya continued to look despondent.

"Okay," he said. "What is it?"

McCoy took a deep breath. "I took your advice and stopped in to see Lieutenant Caan at Security." A bare hint of smile passed over his lips. "It was interesting. I saw the video. We discussed your case further. She had some keen insights, and I think Samarra is convinced you're not the perpetrator of these shenanigans."

"Samarra," repeated Kirk, smiling.

Now McCoy smiled too. But the smile disappeared quickly.

Kirk nodded. "But?"

"But . . . in accordance with Starfleet regulations regarding ongoing investigations, you're grounded until further notice," said McCoy.

It took a moment to sink in.

Then Kirk said: "Grounded?"

McCoy nodded yes.

"You mean I'm banned from Zeta," said Kirk.

"I'm sorry, Jim."

Kirk's head was pounding again. He closed his eyes, rubbing his temples.

T'Laya gently rubbed his shoulders.

"This sucks," she said.

As Kirk slid his arm around her, he heard someone push through the lecture hall doors. It was Uhura.

"Hey," she called. "Is something wrong? You people look like you're at a funeral."

"Jim's grounded," said McCoy. "No Zeta for him."

Uhura looked astounded. "But that's not fair," she protested.

"No, but it's regulation," said McCoy.

Uhura sat in the row behind the others. After a few seconds of silence, she said: "Did anybody find anything?"

T'Laya turned. "Nobody saw him in my quadrant," she said to Uhura.

McCoy shook his head and said, "No witnesses for me either, but I did have a nice talk with Lieutenant Caan. She has some leads."

T'Laya narrowed her eyes. "Yeah, I'll *bet* she does," she said.

Then Kirk raised his hand. "I was with Pavel Chekov," he said.

McCoy widened his eyes. "What? You're joking again, right?"

Kirk shook his head. "He's a really good kid," he said. "Very smart. He's some kind of computer whiz too. He and some geek buddies are trying to trace the infectious agent that attacked his room."

T'Laya sat up straight. She said, "The kid is a genius, I've heard."

Kirk's eyes glazed a bit. He said, "He found like a zillion files that some searchbot stole, including *all* of my Starfleet personnel records." He snickered. "He said that someone has enough information to recreate me if they wanted to. Can you imagine, two of me?" As Kirk talked, his words slurred ever so slightly.

Uhura leaned forward. "Kirk, you don't sound good."

"I agree," said McCoy. "Jim, let's get you to an ICU exam room."

T'Laya wrapped both hands around Kirk's arm and helped him up. Her Vulcan strength surprised him.

"Wow," said Kirk, smiling. Then he frowned. "Wait. Uhura, did *you* find any witnesses?"

Uhura nodded. "Actually, I did."

Kirk brightened. "Who?"

"Let's get you to Medical first," she said.

Minutes later Kirk sat on a white hospital bed.

He was vaguely aware of another presence. It seemed to be next to him. But when he turned to look, nobody was there. He heard his friend Bones talking. Bones was like the older brother he missed. Then he saw Sam, his brother, walking.

"Sam," said Kirk. But Sam kept walking.

Kirk slid to the floor and then stood at the green curtain that circled the white bed.

I'll meet you there shortly, said somebody.

Kirk looked around again. Nobody.

Go now, said the voice. *Before they notice.*

Kirk heard Bones again. He heard Uhura. Then he heard T'Laya. They were his friends, talking beyond the green curtain. But this voice was different.

Kirk slid through the curtain on the side opposite the others and then left the ICU through the main exit, nodding at the check-in nurse as he passed her. She smiled back warmly. In just seconds he was under the black sky rippled with stars. He gazed up as he walked. He even closed his eyes.

His feet knew where to go.

When he was a boy, Kirk did this often: walked with his eyes closed.

Why? asked a voice.

"I liked the way it felt," said Kirk.

How did it feel?

"It made old places feel new," said Kirk, and suddenly that feeling infused him again. "Our yard or the kitchen. Anywhere, really."

Was it a feeling of discovery?

Kirk shrugged. "I guess it was."

Now Kirk felt something else. It was an old fear.

What is it?

Kirk opened his eyes. He glanced back. Dark figures were following him.

T'Laya used a stylus pen to mark the Starfleet Academy campus map displayed on the touchscreen in the ICU nurse station.

"So, he was possibly spotted right here?" she asked.

Standing next to her, Uhura nodded. "Yeah, that's the spot."

"It doesn't tell us much," said T'Laya, frustrated.

Dr. McCoy stood behind her with his arms folded impatiently.

"No, it doesn't," he said. "Look, ladies, all this speculation has been *fascinating*, but I've got a patient to attend to."

Uhura had met a cadet who knew Kirk—a female, of course—and had seen him the night he disappeared. He was standing knee-deep in the fountain in front of the Command College simulator lab. According to the cadet, Kirk was shivering and looked drunk. She had approached him, but he received a communicator call—although, oddly, he answered but didn't speak. Then he hung up and walked away.

"She's sure it was Jim?" asked T'Laya.

Uhura gave her a wry look, and then opened up her notepad.

"They went out a couple of times. Her exact words were: 'After the, uh, *expletive deleted* didn't call me back last time, I spent a couple of weeks hunting him down.'" Uhura pursed her lips. "Then she asked if I knew his room number."

T'Laya grinned. "I hope you gave it to her."

McCoy rolled his eyes. "I'll let you girls finish up your analysis," he said. "I need to get some biosensors on Jim now."

T'Laya quickly touched his arm.

"Dr. McCoy, you've known Jim, what, almost a full year now," she said.

McCoy nodded. "We met on the recruit shuttle, first day."

"You're good friends."

"What do you need to know?" he asked impatiently.

T'Laya looked him in the eye.

"Why is Kirk in Starfleet?" she asked.

McCoy opened a sterile drawer in the nurse station and used a pair of medical tongs to extract a few biosensor patches.

Then he said, "You don't know?"

"He won't give me a straight answer," she said. "I mean,

let's face it—he doesn't fit the standard cadet profile."

McCoy paused. "No, he doesn't," he said. "But, being a Starfleet cadet yourself, you know that ours isn't a standard military mission. We're a peacekeeping, humanitarian armada. We serve in the name of exploration and science."

"But we fight, too," said T'Laya.

"If the Romulans come again, yes, we will fight," said McCoy. "Unless of course they come in peace."

McCoy tapped a button on the station screen. Kirk's latest medical tricorder readouts appeared. T'Laya watched, and then her gray eyes began flitting rapidly as she scanned.

"Are you okay?" asked McCoy, shifting the tricorder to obscure the readings from her line of sight. It was an involuntary action on his part.

T'Laya blinked in embarrassment. "Sorry," she said. "It's my training."

McCoy nodded, feeling a little embarrassed himself. Clearly Jim cared about this girl and she about him. "Anyway, I'm sure you've heard about the USS *Kelvin*."

"Every cadet knows about the *Kelvin*," she replied.

"That was Jim's dad, you know."

"I know."

"Well, then that's probably *all* you need to know," said McCoy.

"Does he want revenge?" asked T'Laya.

McCoy looked surprised. "Against who?"

"Romulans," said T'Laya.

McCoy frowned. "Jim doesn't operate like that."

"But they killed his father," she said.

Now McCoy leaned closer. He repeated: "Jim doesn't operate like that."

T'Laya folded her arms across her chest, watching McCoy arrange the biosensors on a tray. As he was about to slip through the curtain to Kirk's bed, she touched his arm again.

McCoy stopped. "What else, Cadet?"

"Thanks, Leonard."

He smiled. "We're in the ICU," he said. "Please call me Dr. McCoy."

And then he yanked open the curtain to find an empty white bed.

"Good god, he's gone again!" he cried.

Uhura and T'Laya both jumped to their feet. T'Laya immediately sprinted toward the main entrance.

"Where can he be?" she called.

Uhura followed. "He can't be far!"

T'Laya pointed as she ran. "I'll take the route to the dorms. You check that fountain by the Command College. Maybe he'll go back there."

"Good plan," called Uhura.

McCoy grabbed his med-kit.

"Keep in touch!" he shouted. "Jim is not well, and I'm the guy with the medicine."

McCoy trotted behind the two women until they both burst through the Medical College main entrance and veered off in opposite directions. Then he stopped. He waited until they were gone.

"I don't like this," he muttered.

He flipped open his communicator. The line was already open to Security. It had been open the past hour.

"Anybody there?"

A male voice crackled. "Copy."

"Well, he's on the run," said McCoy angrily.

"Roger that," said the voice. "We've got him marked. He's moving fast."

McCoy gritted his teeth.

"Damn it!" he exclaimed. "He's not in good shape. He needs medical attention. I shouldn't have agreed to this scheme. I'm a doctor, not a spy."

"Noted," said the voice. "Don't worry. Dark Angel won't let him run long."

"You'd better not," hissed McCoy. "He won't last. McCoy out."

He flipped the communicator shut. It beeped. He flipped it back open.

"McCoy," he said.

There was a pause. Then: "We lost him, Doctor," said the voice.

"What?" thundered McCoy.

The voice sounded sheepish. "Well, he . . . jumped into a maintenance culvert by National Cemetery."

"So?"

There was a pause. "He must have a map of the underground culvert system. It's very, uh . . . well, we've got two guys lost in there."

"Unbelievable," said McCoy.

He hung up and sprinted out of the building. San Francisco National Cemetery was directly adjacent to the Medical College grounds.

"Never trust a spook," he muttered as he ran.

Kirk knelt on one knee.

"I'm tired," he said.

Nobody answered.

He looked around; he was alone. Then his communicator buzzed in his pocket.

He flipped it open and said, "Kirk here."

A stream of jabbering sound played: clicks, buzzes, beeps. Computer talk. He held the receiver tight to his ear until the transmission ended. Then he flipped the communicator shut.

Change of venue, said somebody.

Kirk nodded. He tried to stand. "I'm on my way. But I'm . . . I'm pretty tired."

They're coming, Mr. Kirk.

Kirk fell. He rolled over onto his back. He lay in a shallow puddle of cold water.

"Yeah, I'll be careful," said Kirk.

For twenty minutes he'd been following the inexplicable bright green line that guided him through the maintenance tunnels. But when he reached the ladder to climb out, his hands would not grip the rungs.

Gazing up the vertical exit pipe from on his back, Kirk could see a circle of stars above. Oddly, he knew them all: He knew which six had planets. He knew Gliese 251, the nearest, just eighteen light-years away. Mekbuda, the supergiant with its radius sixty times solar. Castor and Pollux, the two brightest, the twins. He knew it was Gemini.

He pointed up. "You're a hell of a constellation," he said.

I'm close, said a voice.

Kirk sat bolt upright. It was T'Laya.

"Where are you?" he asked, looking around.

Close, she said. *Climb up the pipe.*

"Okay."

He struggled to his feet and then put his hands on the first ladder rungs. The back of his clothes and hair were soaking wet. But the thought of reaching T'Laya gave him a burst of energy. He climbed slowly but steadily to the top and rolled out of the pipe.

"Where are you?" he called, looking around.

Now nobody answered.

Kirk staggered to his feet.

A gentle dark hill rose away from the culvert. Perfect rows of ghost-white markers lined the slope. He was in National Cemetery.

Now he saw figures, dark and crouched, gliding through the grave markers. They seemed to move impossibly fast. Kirk started to run. But it felt like he was running in water.

They're coming for you, said T'Laya behind him.

Kirk spun around.

"Where *are* you?" he called, spinning.

We have to shut it down, she said. *I'm sorry.*

Kirk ran again. He heard light footfalls. Behind him, a slender figure emerged from the front rank of grave markers. Its movements seemed preternatural: He saw cobalt wings, talons, a dark avenging angel. He sprinted for a battery of lights up ahead. But when he reached the perimeter security fence—a fence he knew he could not scale—and he spun to face his pursuer, the killer angel stopped and held out one of her palms.

She said, "Stop running, Mr. Kirk."

Kirk said, "Why?"

It was Samarra Caan, of course. She raised a phaser and slowly aimed.

"Sit down," she said. "Make this easier for both of us."

"Easier?" repeated Kirk.

Lieutenant Caan calmly prepared to fire.

Kirk looked up and slowly closed his eyes. In the sky, the bright twins, Castor and Pollux, flickered . . . and then went black.

When Gemini hailed Nverinn requesting an Alpha-level security link, he felt his throat tighten. His protection array of gridbots had just shut down forty-one more subspace frequencies. Somebody was poking around and had made inroads. Somebody with brilliant computer skills. His agent was playing pure defense now.

But his scans showed none of the usual heavy-handed Starfleet signatures. This counterattack was original, probably coming from an individual source, and it was light on its feet.

And now here was Gemini.

This was not good.

The first contact was a simple hailing sequence: Gemini's request. Nverinn opened an infrared Alpha frequency band and then moved his fingers to the touch keyboard. No voice contact now: too time-consuming to encode, and damning evidence if somehow intercepted.

Nverinn typed: *What's going on?*

It took a full thirty seconds for the encryption and transmission. Nverinn braced for a slow, frustrating, and perhaps disturbing exchange.

After thirty seconds more, the reply arrived: *Second infection shut down. Subject has been compromised.*

He typed: *Where and how are you?*

The next message made him smile. It read simply: *Safe and sound.*

As Nverinn prepared to type again, another message appeared: *Gemini database secure but searchnet detected. Expect countermeasures.*

He nodded. That was already happening.

Then he typed: *Status of subject?*

The wait was almost two full minutes for this reply: *Subject down.*

Nverinn stared at the words. *Down?*

He typed: *Clarify, please.*

But just seconds after he sent this, another Gemini message popped up: *Possible termination. Events unfolding, must sign off. Gemini out.*

Nverinn felt a chill of dread.

Gemini had been trained to terminate the project without hesitation if detection seemed imminent. But terminating the *subject*—that was for extreme circumstance only.

Nverinn wondered if Gemini was conflicted. The program gave her full override on all functional decisions. But how would she proceed on this one?

He bowed his head and whispered, *"Farr Jolan,* Mr. Kirk. Peace awaits."

CH.11.13
Heschl's Gyrus

Spock leaned against a tree.

He wasn't used to standing around aimlessly, and he was slightly embarrassed as cadets passed, including several students and ex-students who nodded respectfully. But his purpose was real and considerable.

So he waited.

Finally, Cadet Uhura exited the Medical College. She was in a hurry.

"Commander!" she said, surprised.

Spock looked down, then smiled. *Yes,* he thought. *We are indeed in uniform.*

"How is your friend, Cadet?" he asked.

"Good, I think," she said. "Still unconscious when I left. But the doctor says his readings are stable and normalizing."

"Good to hear," said Spock. "I will walk with you."

"Great!" said Uhura. "Please do."

Spock fell in beside her, and they moved briskly along the central promenade.

"I need your help," said Spock bluntly.

Uhura smiled. "My help?" she said. "I'm your student. I don't help, I follow orders."

Bemused, Spock took a few more strides before he spoke again.

"Starfleet Intelligence has intercepted subspace transmissions," he said. "Just fragments, most of which do not make sense. It is hard to tell if they are encrypted or just gibberish. But the outflow volume seems significant, with the transmissions routing into the Neutral Zone."

"Outflow?" repeated Uhura. "From where?"

Spock knitted his brow. "Here," he said.

"Earth?"

"So it seems," he said.

Uhura raised her eyebrows. "*That's* rather disturbing," she said.

"Yes," said Spock. "Thus Intelligence has given our study a Code Tango priority. And you now have Level Six security clearance."

Uhura smiled. "Wow," she said. "I feel important."

Spock nodded but said nothing.

"So you think it's Romulan," said Uhura.

"Yes, I believe that is a strong possibility," replied Spock. "Even encrypted Romulan can have recognizable phonology, as you know, so I need your ear. Being as it is far more gifted than mine."

Uhura smiled, thinking: *You need my ear.*

"Well, that's a start," she said.

Spock arched a puzzled eyebrow.

Uhura continued down the promenade at a brisk pace. She seemed exhilarated, and Spock suddenly noticed that other cadets were striding with a similar sense of purpose, all in the same direction. So Spock finally asked, "If I may ask, Cadet . . . where is everybody going?"

Uhura gave Spock a shocked look.

"Commander!" she said. "It's Zeta day."

Spock looked puzzled again.

"But, Cadet," he said. "You already *know* your Zeta assignment. I revealed it to you."

"Sure," she said, walking faster. "But I want to know where everybody *else* ends up!"

Kirk woke in the ICU again, with another IV drip in his arm. Lingering images swirled: tunnel, sky, dark angel with a phaser. His head felt like a rotting melon. A concerned McCoy was staring down at him.

"Bones, I love these beds," mumbled Kirk. "Can I have one?"

McCoy grinned and took a relieved breath.

"You should just move in here," said the doctor.

Kirk nodded. "By now I should have my own wing," he said.

The curtain around his bed pulled back, and Lieutenant Caan stepped in beside McCoy. Kirk's eyes widened.

Caan's cool gaze settled on Kirk. "How is he, Leonard?" she asked.

"Have a look," said McCoy, gesturing at Kirk.

Kirk pointed at her. "You *shot* me!" he exclaimed.

"Yes, she did," said McCoy. He turned to Lieutenant Caan. "Thank you, Samarra, for overcoming your well-trained instincts and setting for stun rather than killing this bozo."

"Killing Mr. Kirk would be bad for Starfleet," she said with a smile.

"I suppose so," said McCoy.

Kirk tried to sit up, but a Velcro strap across his chest held him down.

"Bones, why am I strapped to this bed?" he said.

McCoy reached under the bed and unfastened the strap.

"Precautionary," he said. "You suffered a series of violent seizures when we first brought you in. Frankly, it scared the hell out of me."

"Seizures?" Kirk sat up. Then he winced in pain, laying back down. "Wow, that hurts."

Lieutenant Caan watched McCoy adjust the IV drip. "You're lucky that Dr. McCoy was with my team when we caught up to you," she said.

Kirk exhaled slowly and stared up at the ceiling.

"So what's happening to me, Bones?" he asked.

McCoy waved his trusty tricorder.

"We're not entirely sure yet," he said. "But I have some ideas. We found traces of something. Whatever's in your system didn't have time to fully dissipate this time. I've got the lab working on it." Then something struck him. "Wait a minute!" He eyed Kirk. "Jim . . . you *remember* Samarra shooting you with her phaser?"

"Yes, I do," said Kirk, wincing.

Lieutenant Caan produced her notebook. "Do you remember anything else, Mr. Kirk?" she asked.

Kirk blinked slowly.

"Not sure," he said. "A few images. Like a dream." He met her blue gaze. "They seem unreal."

"Tell me everything you remember," said Caan.

"Well, stars, for one," said Kirk. "I looked at the sky, and it was like a planetarium." He stared at the ceiling again, remembering. "I knew every constellation and cluster, every star's name. Like a star chart was overlaid on the sky."

Lieutenant Caan raised her eyebrows, exchanging a look with McCoy.

"Okay," said Kirk, a bit embarrassed. "So maybe *that* part was a dream."

"Maybe not, Jim," said McCoy. "Listen. This thing, this . . . *infection*, for lack of a better word—I think it some-how gave you a heightened sense of perception. I say this because of some things you've told me over the past twelve hours."

Kirk tried to sit up again. "I've been here *twelve hours*?" he exclaimed.

"Yep," said McCoy, pushing him back down.

"And I've been talking?" asked Kirk.

"On and off," said McCoy.

"What did I say?" asked Kirk.

"Among other things, you expressed concern about a dark angel," said McCoy.

Kirk squinted. "It was following me," he said.

Lieutenant Caan rested her hands on the edge of the bed and said, "That was me, Mr. Kirk."

"Yesterday, I asked Lieutenant Caan to put you under protective surveillance," said McCoy.

"I tried to be your *guardian* angel," she said. "But you slipped away."

"I saw subtle signs of relapse and thought you might bolt again," continued McCoy. He nodded toward Samarra. "So I contacted Samarra. Our first plan was to keep you in medical custody. But her brilliant superiors over at

Intelligence wanted to let you go, hoping you'd lead them to whoever was manipulating you."

"Then you eluded our entire team in that insidious maze," said Lieutenant Caan.

"What maze?" asked Kirk.

"The maintenance culverts, Jim," said McCoy.

Kirk looked confused. "The tunnel?"

McCoy chuckled. "More like a hundred tunnels. They connect everything in the Presidio."

The Presidio, originally established as a Spanish garrison in 1776, eventually became a large United States Army headquarters in 1847. The Army Corps of Engineers installed an elaborate underground maintenance system to connect the base in case of siege. Three hundred years later, the culverts still existed. They survived the Great Earthquakes of 1906 and 2182.

"I'm curious, Mr. Kirk," said Lieutenant Caan. "How did you get through so fast? Two of our agents got lost for nearly an hour."

Kirk frowned.

"I just followed the glowing green line," he said.

Samarra looked confused. "You saw a line?"

McCoy raised a finger.

"See? That's what I mean," he said to Lieutenant Caan. "It's almost as if this infection did something to his brain— rewired it or laid new neural pathways." He turned to

Kirk. "Somehow, it gave you information and guidance—apparently even *visual* guidance."

Kirk's memory stirred. "It talked to me too," he said.

"Really?" McCoy was intrigued.

"Yeah, there were voices," said Kirk. "Telling me where to go."

"Interesting," said McCoy.

Kirk grinned wryly at McCoy. "So I'm crazy, too, right?"

"Maybe. But maybe not."

McCoy quickly adjusted some settings on his medical tricorder and then started waving it around Kirk's head again.

"What are you doing now, Bones?" asked Kirk.

"Scanning your Heschl's Gyrus," said McCoy.

"Good," said Kirk. "It's been itching lately."

McCoy ignored the joke, concentrating on the scan. As he did, Samarra's communicator beeped.

"This is Lieutenant Caan," she answered. She listened for a few seconds, then said: "I'm on my way."

"We'll miss you," said Kirk, turning to her as she hung up. "Well, he will for sure," he added, pointing to McCoy.

"Don't move, please," said McCoy through gritted teeth.

Lieutenant Caan looked at McCoy. "They want my report," she said wryly.

McCoy smiled up at her.

"Give 'em hell, sugar," he said.

"Oh, I will," she said. She put her hand lightly on his shoulder. "Good luck, Leonard." Then she looked at Kirk. "Stay put, Mr. Kirk."

Kirk gave her a wave.

"Stop moving!" repeated McCoy.

As Samarra ducked out through the bed curtain, Kirk eyed McCoy sideways.

"Bones, talk to me," he said.

"Heschl's Gyrus is a ridge on the temporal lobe of your brain that processes auditory stimuli," said McCoy. "It lets you hear things."

"That's not what I mean." Kirk grinned.

McCoy examined readouts on the tricorder. He didn't speak for a second. Then he said, "I like her."

Kirk's grin broadened. "She likes you, too," he said.

Now McCoy scowled. "And if you say anything more, the whole thing will be jinxed."

He held up his tricorder.

"These readings, Jim," he said. "They may explain those voices you're hearing."

"I'm all ears," said Kirk.

McCoy gave him a sour smile. "Schizophrenics 'hear' voices in their heads because of a neurological quirk," he said. "To put it simply, one part of the schizophrenic's brain—the part that generates speech—literally 'talks' to the part that *hears* speech, the transverse temporal ridge, also called Heschl's Gyrus. Now, we *all* have interior conversations with ourselves, to some extent. But because of abnormalities in a schizophrenic temporal lobe, the schizoid hearer can't fully distinguish internal from external stimuli. So his brain processes the inner voices as real sound."

"Bones, if you're trying to tell me I'm crazy . . ." Kirk shook his head. "I readily admit that I am."

"The brain scans I did immediately after Samarra stunned you show an *amazing* amount of metabolic activity in that gyrus of your brain," said McCoy. "The same goes for your visual cortex, the brain area that receives information from the lateral geniculate body of the thalamus."

Kirk rolled his eyes.

"Speak English to me, man," he said.

"This infection is making you see and hear things, Jim," said McCoy. "But not random things that your brain just generates, like a schizophrenic episode. The information *you're* processing—the stuff you're seeing and hearing— seems to have a specific purpose. A *guiding* purpose. For example: It probably tricked your vision into seeing a preset path, a glowing line through a maze of culverts." He shook his head. "Incredible! It's almost like somebody uploaded neurological code into your head."

"Like brain software?" said Kirk.

"Exactly."

Kirk shook his head. "Wow."

McCoy gave him a sharp look. "Jim, this thing *can't* be a mere infection. It's either a sentient, intelligent entity itself, or it's an ingenious tool being directed by someone else."

Kirk couldn't help it. He started feeling around the curve of his skull.

"Is it alive, do you think?" he asked.

"Not exactly, but we'll know more when we get the lab results," said McCoy. "I do expect a totally organic, carbon-based molecular structure."

"Why?" asked Kirk.

"Because it dissipates so quickly," said McCoy. "It must be encoded with a self-destruct mechanism, allowing it to simply break down into component molecules that just absorb right into the host's system. It leaves no trace of its existence other than the residual metabolic reactions of your brain and immune system."

A buzzer sounded on the station console. McCoy tapped a button. As he did so, Kirk noticed the time on the display screen: 0842.

"Twelve hours," muttered Kirk. "That's nuts." Suddenly his eyes lit up: *It's Friday!*

He spun to McCoy. "Is the Zeta list up?"

When McCoy hesitated, Kirk held up his hands.

"Bones, I know I'm grounded," he said. "I do remember that. So what's your assignment?"

McCoy sighed. "*Farragut*," he said.

"Chief medical officer?" asked Kirk.

"Yeah."

Kirk whooped and whacked McCoy on the arm. "Not bad for a Mississippi bootlegger!" His head seemed lighter. "What about the girls?"

McCoy leveled a cheerless look at Kirk.

"*Farragut*," he said again.

Kirk howled. "Son of a buck, that's sweet. Is Uhura on the bridge?"

"What do *you* think?" asked McCoy.

"I think, hell yes, she's on the bridge," said Kirk. He suddenly felt great. "And T'Laya? Let me guess. Upper engineering deck. She's running the computer bay."

"That is correct," said McCoy.

"Who's the chief engineer?" asked Kirk.

"Olsen," said McCoy.

Kirk nodded and grinned. "Excellent," he said. "I'll have fun monitoring you guys from mission control. And, Bones, they'd better put me on the mission comm-desk or I'll have to—"

"Jim," interrupted McCoy.

"What?"

"Hold still and listen." McCoy slid the IV needle from

Kirk's right arm, then taped a wad of gauze over the spot. "I've got good news . . . and bad news."

Kirk nodded. "I'm ready, man."

"It's pretty clear, even to the geniuses at Starfleet Intelligence, that you didn't sabotage Cadet Chekov's room," said McCoy. "And a cursory review of your alleged Honor Code violations—lying, cheating—well, they all seem dubious at best. *You* saw them. Whoever drummed those up did a pretty sloppy job."

Kirk nodded. "They seem like a smokescreen. But for what, I have no idea."

"The lieutenant agrees with that assessment," said McCoy. He started peeling biosensor patches from Kirk's left arm. "The charges weren't meant to stick. Some are downright ludicrous . . . to anyone who knows you, anyway. So Samarra had a little chat with the commandant, and to make a long story short, you've been assigned to the USS *Farragut* along with the rest of us."

Kirk grinned. He couldn't speak.

"However," said McCoy. "We have no definitive medical explanation yet for your episodes. So you'll be under strict observation by Lieutenant Caan during the entire exercise."

Kirk shrugged. "That's not so bad," he said.

"Well, that's not really the bad news," said McCoy. "Given the ongoing uncertainty of your condition, the commandant couldn't assign you a captaincy, obviously. So your post is first officer, exercise rank of lieutenant commander. Your station is Security."

"Security," said Kirk, nodding as he processed the news. "Okay."

The first officer, also known as executive officer, or XO, was second-in-command on a typical starship. The XO was typically responsible for logistics and maintenance, freeing the captain to concentrate on tactical planning and execution. The XO also had a station assignment, which could vary. Some first officers doubled as the ship's science officer. In Kirk's case, he would oversee the ship's onboard security and any tactical away-team operations.

Kirk rubbed his arm. "Well, at least I'm aboard, I guess," he said. "It could be worse."

"That's true, it could be worse," said McCoy. "For example, the *Farragut*'s captain could be Viktor Tikhonov."

Kirk just stared at McCoy.

After a few seconds, he said: "No way."

"I'm afraid so," said McCoy. "And *there's* your bad news."

Kirk groaned and then lay back again.

"However," added McCoy, "here's some more *good* news. I'm releasing you to your room for twenty-four hours of prescribed rest."

Kirk sat back up. "Thanks, Bones," he said.

"Sure," said McCoy with a funny-looking grin. "But you're not out of the woods, friend. I'll be checking on you and running scans periodically. And I've assigned you a personal attendant."

He yanked open the bed curtain. Curled up and dozing on a chair sat T'Laya.

Kirk fought the urge to leap out of bed.

"She's been here since the moment we brought you in," McCoy told him. "She didn't want to leave your side."

McCoy gently poked T'Laya's shoulder and she woke.

Then she smiled at Kirk.

"Hey, Lieutenant Commander," she said. "Let's party."

CH.12.13
Zeta Launch

Kirk was awakened by a bright slash of sunlight across his face. Squinting in annoyance, he rolled over to see a shapely silhouette at the window, surrounded by a halo of morning sunburst.

"Up, Cadet," called T'Laya.

Kirk groaned. "Isn't it Saturday?"

"There is no weekend in Starfleet," she replied. "Especially Zeta weekend."

"Yeah, yeah," said Kirk, slinging his legs out of the bed.

"Come on, get up," said T'Laya. "Your first *Farragut* bridge team meeting is at 0900." She stepped out of the glare. She was wearing his XXL Iowa Hawkeye T-shirt as a nightshirt. "Let's get dressed, then grab some breakfast."

Kirk staggered to his feet and then wrapped her up in a hug.

"Not hungry," he said.

"Dr. McCoy says you need to eat to build your strength." She rested her hands on his hips.

"All I need is a snack," he said, grinning.

"Not now," she insisted, gently pushing him away. "Don't you want to make a good first impression on your commanding officer, Captain Tikhonov?"

Kirk grimaced.

"Okay, that hurt," he said.

"Remember what you told me, Mr. Kirk," said T'Laya as she gathered up her things. "'You don't win with a playbook. You win with people.'"

"When did I tell you that?" he asked.

T'Laya's eyes jittered on recall for a second. Then she blinked.

"Oh, that first night we met," she said. "At the Perihelion. You went on and on about teamwork. Team this, team that."

"Huh," said Kirk, trying to remember and unable to. "That was the lost night, I guess."

"Come on, get dressed," said T'Laya, suddenly changing the subject. "I want some French toast."

And thus began the cyclonic fury of term-end week.

First-year cadets either caught the cyclone's wind and soared, or curled up low to ride out the storm. The schedule was rigged to minimize introspection, sleep, catch-up, or second-guessing. You were either prepared and fit for duty, or you weren't.

Kirk's final exams were in Tactical Analysis, Fleet Dynamics, Bridge Operations and Protocol, and Fleet Command and Control Methods. Although his pre-Academy aptitude tests were off the charts—Captain Pike had once called him "the only genius-level repeat offender in the Midwest"—he was still learning how to modulate the intensity level expected of Starfleet officer candidates without burning out.

Fortunately, Kirk had the perfect role model that week.

T'Laya was an incredibly focused worker. But she knew how to counter stress too. They studied together for hours and attended the *Farragut* crew orientation and simulator training sessions, yet still found time to hunt down cheap native-style Cantonese takeout in Chinatown. T'Laya's inherited Vulcan physical strength made other activities interesting too.

McCoy checked in less and less frequently as the week wore on. He felt confident that he was in good hands with T'Laya. Plus, Kirk had no more episodes, and he seemed to feel stronger each day.

As for Captain Viktor Tikhonov: Kirk studiously maintained a low profile at *Farragut* bridge officer meetings and in the simulators. It wasn't easy: Other cadets were well aware of the rivalry, and Tikhonov wasn't shy about asserting his superior position. But Kirk focused on his station duties and took Viktor's orders with good humor.

It helped knowing he had T'Laya to look forward to each evening.

Whenever Kirk fulfilled the first officer's standard role of offering advice to the captain, he kept the discussion private, and he stuck to personnel issues. Kirk knew many of the *Farragut* cadets better than Tikhonov, and quietly recommended ways to better manage and mesh their personalities.

To Tikhonov's credit, he seemed to welcome Kirk's input on such matters. But the Russian was uncompromising on tactical matters. In fleet maneuver scenarios on the simulated bridge, Viktor barked orders that he expected his bridge officers to simply follow without discussion or input.

Kirk found this particularly frustrating: The Russian's dogged relentlessness was his strength in smaller tactical scenarios. But in larger-scale fleet action, Tikhonov's reluctance to disengage from an exchange and try a fresh approach sometimes hurt him. In their earlier simulator battles, Kirk's victories over Tikhonov were often the result of taking creative, flexible, and unexpected courses of action.

For seven straight days, the wicked pace continued: exam, training, exam, training. But at the end Kirk felt curiously energized and ready to go. A brief exchange with T'Laya over a midnight glass of wine in his room also put his mind at ease.

It was the eve of Zeta launch. They'd just learned that day that the exercise was officially dubbed Operation Titan Storm.

As they clinked together their glasses, Kirk said, "To Captain Tikhonov."

"May he reign forever," said T'Laya.

They drank. Then T'Laya stood, carrying her goblet to the window.

"Lights," she said loudly.

"Lights off," replied the room computer. The room lights slowly dimmed to black.

"I have to leave soon, but first I want to see the stars," she said.

Kirk joined her at the window. He pointed toward two bright points of light, high in the northern sky.

"I happen to know now that Castor and Pollux are the twin stars of Gemini," he said. "I didn't know that a week ago. I know a lot more too, but it would make your head explode."

T'Laya set her wine goblet on the sill.

"Oh, I know my constellations," she said.

"Let's see, which way is Saturn?" asked Kirk, putting down his goblet too.

"There," said T'Laya, pointing.

"Wow, you do know your sky," said Kirk, impressed. He followed her gaze. "Hard to believe we'll be there in, like, nine hours."

T'Laya suddenly faced him, grabbed his shirt collar with both hands, and pressed her lips onto his. He widened his eyes in delight, and he was about to ease into the kiss when she broke off and stared hard at him. Her eyes were just inches from his.

"Listen to me," she said.

He smiled at her intensity. "Okay," he said.

"Whatever happens tomorrow will be good for you," she said. "Win or lose."

"I prefer win," he said.

"I know you don't believe in no-win scenarios," she said.

"When did I tell you that?" asked Kirk.

"You tell everybody that," she said.

"That's true."

"The thing is, I agree," said T'Laya. "As long as you do the right thing, as you see it in your heart, then you win." She still gripped his collar. "The ones who care for you— the ones who count—they will always know. That's the ultimate power in the galaxy."

Kirk nodded in admiration.

"Hey, I like that," he said. "I like it a lot." He grinned. "Of course I'm with you, so my judgment is impaired."

T'Laya quickly lowered her eyes. Then she closed them as tears began to flow.

"Man, you Vulcans can be really *weepy* sometimes," said Kirk.

T'Laya's tearful snort got them both laughing.

"My nose is running like a spigot," she said.

"Here, use my sleeve."

She snorted again, and they both started laughing hysterically. Kirk suddenly playfully pulled her to the nearby bed and settled next to her. T'Laya buried her face in a pillow. Kirk thought she was still laughing but quickly realized that she was sobbing uncontrollably. Kirk stroked her back, unsure what to say.

"Wow," he said. "I guess you're really stressed about tomorrow . . . ?" he ventured. Crying girls made him uncomfortable.

"I don't *get* this." She moaned into the pillow.

"Me neither," said Kirk. "This is what I get for serving wine to minors."

She laughed again and managed to catch a breath, then dropped the pillow.

"I didn't think I'd like you so much," she said.

"Well, you're ruined for life now," he said.

"I think that's probably true." She looked away. "I can never do *this* again, that's for sure."

"Do what again?" asked Kirk.

"Lights!" called T'Laya, shaking herself out of her reverie.

"Lights on," said a computer voice, and the room lights slowly brightened.

T'Laya jumped up to nab the wine goblets. As she handed Kirk his, she said, "One last toast."

Kirk took his goblet, then raised it.

T'Laya said, "I'd like to propose a toast to the ironic fact that whoever controls a starship's engineering computer bay is the person who *actually* controls the starship."

Kirk grinned. They clinked goblets.

He said, "I really do like the way you think."

T'Laya took a swallow of pinot noir and then said, "Keep that in mind, Mr. Kirk, when the *Farragut*'s captain rushes in for the kill-shot on a ship that he mistakenly thinks he's crippled."

Kirk nodded, impressed again.

"I'll keep that in mind," he said, and drank.

"Seriously, keep your thumb on that guy," said T'Laya. "He scares me. He'll trigger a galactic incident someday, probably a war."

"Viktor is a warrior, first and last." Kirk nodded. "If he ever gets outmaneuvered, I guarantee you, he'd rather go out guns blazing than make a crafty tactical withdrawal."

T'Laya smiled sadly at the suggestion, and then seemed to clear the thought from her head.

"Well, I've established *excellent* rapport with my boss, Chief Engineer Olsen," she said. "Let's just say that Engineering will pay close attention to any suggestions that might trickle down from the first officer's command station."

Kirk said, "I'll take that under advisement."

He took her wine goblet and set both down.

"Well," he said. "I have to report to the Shuttle Hangar at 0600."

T'Laya nodded. "I'm leaving. We both need some rest," she said, pulling on her coat. "Remember what I said about tomorrow."

"Hey, I'll see you in the morning, okay?" Kirk replied as he pulled her in for a good-bye kiss.

T'Laya didn't respond. She simply kissed him back and then slipped out the door.

Ten hours later, the USS *Farragut* NCC-1647 dropped out of warp into the shadow of Saturn. In seconds the rest of Task Force Blue popped soundlessly out of warp space around its flagship, arriving in delta formation: four Saladin-class destroyers; four Hermes-class scouts; and an array of support/supply vessels, including some Class-F shuttles and one Antares-type cargo vessel. The larger ships also transported three swift squadrons of Tornado-class training fighters.

From his tactical station, Kirk watched Tikhonov carefully.

Viktor had a firm grasp of the fundamentals of task force command. He expertly brought about the *Farragut*, then systematically deployed the full flotilla in a logical order of battle, just as they'd learned in simulator training.

"Communications!" boomed Tikhonov. His voice dripped with adrenaline.

Kirk glanced over at Uhura, one station over. She smiled back, then turned to the command chair where Tikhonov sat. The bridge stations were arrayed in a circle around that chair, with the helm console directly in front and below.

"Yes, Captain," replied Uhura. "We are within hailing range of Starbase Zeta."

"Hold off on that frequency, Lieutenant," said Tikhonov. "Let's secure the area first."

"All sensors active," called Kirk. "I have a vector lock on Starbase Zeta. Locking . . . now."

On the huge main viewscreen, a green target box locked around a starlike blip hovering outside the planetary rings.

"Fighters away," called Tikhonov.

"All three Tornado squadrons are launched and vectored in," called Hannity, the Operations officer.

Viktor nodded, balling up his fists.

"Give *Farragut* a planet-side screen with Alpha

Squadron," he said. "Get Beta and Gamma Squadrons in an all-points formation around the starbase. I want destroyer pickets forward and aft as well."

"Aye, Captain," said Hannity.

"Gentlemen, we know Task Force Gold is out there," said Tikhonov with a dark look. "So Mr. Kirk, let's plot a likely threat axis."

"You got it," said Kirk.

One hour earlier, while still moored at Starbase 1 (the massive Starfleet docking station in geostationary orbit above Earth), the entire flight roster of Task Force Blue had gotten a preliminary mission briefing on their ships' viewscreens.

The Blue team's primary objective in Operation Titan Storm was to scuttle an orbital platform known as Starbase Zeta. For purposes of the Zeta exercise, the mission facts were as follows:

> Starbase Zeta was an abandoned mining facility circling Saturn's largest moon, Titan. With a length of 560 meters and a mass of 3.1 million metric tons, Zeta was a considerable object.
>
> Starbase Zeta's orbit was in rapid decline. The huge station was expected to reenter

Titan's atmosphere within forty-eight hours and make a fiery descent to the planet's surface.

The moon below, Titan, was designated a densely populated Federation world of more than ten billion inhabitants. Thus Zeta's reentry would likely produce catastrophic results. Millions of Titan lives could be at stake.

(In reality, of course, Titan was an uninhabited moon covered with liquid methane lakes, a surface temperature of minus 259 degrees Fahrenheit, and an unbreathable nitrogen atmosphere.)

Corporate mining interests had abandoned the platform years ago. Now it was a haven for smugglers, Nausicaan pirates, and other low-life scum.

Thus the two mission objectives for Task Force Blue: give the seedy inhabitants time to evacuate, and then vaporize the station using phaser banks. The goal was to create debris small enough to allow complete burn-up on reentry to the atmosphere, preventing a deadly rain of fire on Titan.

Of course, every cadet in Task Force Blue knew that

their counterparts in Task Force Gold had been assigned mission objectives that would somehow conflict with theirs. But nobody knew the details.

That was the fun of the Zeta exercise.

Kirk felt strong tinges of envy now. Things were unfolding rapidly, and Viktor was handling it like a pro. The two Blue team squadrons of Tornado-class fighters shot past the *Farragut* window toward the starbase boxed in green on-screen.

"Helmsman McKenna," Tikhonov called to the pilot at the helm console in front of him. "Get us within targeting range of Zeta."

"Yes, sir," replied McKenna. "Engineering, give me one-quarter impulse burst for four seconds. I'll do the rest with thrusters."

Over the comm, the voice of Chief Engineer Olsen replied, "Aye, helmsman. Ready when you are."

"On my mark . . . now."

As the helm crew maneuvered the massive *Farragut* into position closer to the Zeta platform, Tikhonov slowly rotated the command chair to face Kirk.

"Mr. Kirk," called Tikhonov with a smile. "Do you think we will encounter resistance from Starbase Zeta personnel?"

"Not likely, sir, but you never know," said Kirk.

Tikhonov nodded. "Would you recommend we go to general quarters?"

"Absolutely," replied Kirk.

"Prepare a red alert, then, for all fleet vessels," said Tikonov, rubbing his hand over the command chair status display.

Kirk nodded with a thin smile. A red alert took the crew to general quarters (also called "battle stations")—a prudent move by Captain Tikhonov. What amused Kirk was that red alerts were typically issued by the commanding officer. Kirk had no doubt that his Russian rival was dangling a tantalizing taste of command in front of him, and enjoying it immensely.

A tone sounded, and a face familiar to all cadets suddenly appeared on the main viewscreen.

"Greetings, Task Force Blue, this is acting Fleet Admiral Christopher Pike." He nodded. "Captain Tikhonov. Are you prepared for general quarters?"

"Aye, sir," replied Tikhonov. "All ships of Task Force Blue are at condition yellow, going to red."

"Excellent," said Pike. "Starfleet sensors have indicated an unusual subspace signature on the far side of Saturn." He smiled. "You might want to investigate before you proceed with Starbase Zeta evacuation and demolition."

As *Farragut* and its fleet went to battle stations, Kirk noticed that Lieutenant Samarra Caan was now on the bridge. She stood unobtrusively near McCoy at the Medical station and gave Kirk a nod. As she did, T'Laya's voice crackled quietly on his station's comm-speaker.

Kirk was happy to hear her voice. He'd missed her before boarding, and based on how strangely she'd acted the night before, he'd had a nagging concern she wasn't going to show up. *Which would have been crazy,* he thought now.

"How's it going up there?" she asked.

"Great," murmured Kirk. "It's really fun watching Viktor do everything while I say *'Nothing on sensors, Captain'* over and over again."

"You're head of Security, right?" she whispered.

"Yeah."

"Start a fight," she said.

Kirk snickered. Suddenly, he saw activity on infrared.

"Uh-oh," said Kirk. "Gotta go."

"See ya," whispered T'Laya.

"I've got engines firing up in the Zeta docking bay," he called out to Tikhonov. "Have we hailed the criminals on the platform yet?"

"No, Mr. Kirk," replied Uhura.

"My sensors read these heat signatures as Nausicaan craft, probably Raiders," he called to Tikhonov.

"I'm getting something from Gamma squadron, sir," reported Hannity. "We have activity. Sounds like the pirates are scrambling their fighters."

Tikhonov scoffed. "Surely they don't plan to engage a Federation battle fleet?"

"Making a run for it, more like," said Kirk. He wanted to add: *Just let them go, Viktor. Get ready for Task Force Gold. Pike just told you they're here.*

"Give me squadron leaders," said Tikhonov quickly.

After a second, an excited voice could be heard on the bridge transmission. "Gamma leader here," it said.

"What are the pirates doing?" asked Tikhonov.

"Leaving, sir. Do you want us to give them an exit path?"

Tikhonov scowled. "I want you to shoot them from the sky," he said.

After a pause, Gamma leader replied, "Aye, sir. Attack formation."

"Beta leader here, sir," crackled a voice. "You want us to intercept bogies too?"

"Negative," said Tikhonov. "I want you to hit that starbase docking bay. Let's flush them all out. We can clear the base faster."

Kirk almost bit through his tongue trying not to speak.

Viktor probably thought he was showing impressive initia-
tive: *A few pirates? Who cares?* Clear the base, blow it up.
Meet the objective fast, then go hunt down the Gold fleet.
That was Tikhonov's nature. But in rushing things he might
be taking his eye off the ball.

All the weapons-fire in the war game was virtual fire,
of course. When a ship got tagged, a computerized damage
assessment adjusted the ship's status. Kirk monitored his
sensor scans and listened as the Blue fighters tangled with
Nausicaan Raiders (flown by experienced Starfleet pilots).
Then he heard something that made him look up.

"Beta leader to Farragut, over."

"Go ahead, Beta."

"Looks like we hit some sort of . . . diplomatic shuttle
maybe, in the bay," he said. "I also see a row of big cargo
haulers with Task Force Gold markings. *Lot* of activity
down there, sir."

Kirk couldn't help it.

"Withdraw and hail!" he blurted out. When Tikhonov
and others looked at him, he added, "Uh, is my suggestion . . .
Captain."

"Why, Mr. Kirk?" asked Tikhonov.

"Somebody over there might tell us what's going on,"
said Kirk. "We have overwhelming firepower and forty-
eight hours until the thing falls from the sky. We can afford
to assess carefully."

Tikhonov didn't bother to disguise his contempt for what he considered to be a cowardly course of action.

"Gamma, do not target the shuttle," he said calmly into the comm. "Eliminate all Gold cargo ships. Do you copy?"

"Yes, sir, commencing run."

Tikhonov almost bounced in this chair. He loved to attack. "Beta, continue to engage and pursue all pirate vessels."

"We've lost birds, sir!" cried Beta leader. "Two and five are gone. These guys are *good*."

Kirk was about to speak again, but managed to hold his tongue this time. Undermining Viktor now would be a huge mistake; it would only spur him to be more aggressive. But then Kirk's scanners picked up a single ship's signature. His computer identified it as . . . *Romulan*?

What is going on here? Kirk wondered. The single ship made no sense in this scenario. And it being Romulan just added to the mystery. *Are my sensors malfunctioning?*

He looked over at Uhura. Her eyes were excited.

"Captain, I'm picking up a transmission, a single vessel," she said. "It's encrypted but . . . but I've heard similar chatter recently."

Tikhonov looked exasperated. "So?" he said.

Uhura glanced at Kirk. "I think it may be Romulan."

Kirk was about to support her with his sensor report when suddenly all hell broke loose.

"Captain, this is the *Hannibal*," cried a voice. It was the captain of one of the Saladin-class destroyers. "We've got multiple capital ships to starboard, coming in guns blazing! We're taking heavy—!"

"Shields full!" shouted Tikhonov.

"Already done," answered Kirk, punching buttons.

"Helmsman, get us to starboard!"

"Aye, sir," replied McKenna.

"We've got hostiles to port, too," said Kirk, eyeing his scans. "That's Gold fleet, and they're hitting both flanks at once, Viktor."

"Fire back!" shouted Tikhonov. "Fire at will!"

"Wow, Captain, this is Olsen," reported the chief engineer over the bridge comm. "Engineering is in bad shape down here, sir. We just took bloody direct hits from each side. The simulation computer is taking away our impulse drive."

"Shields at fifty percent!" called McKenna from the helm. "Captain, I'm taking us hard to port, then ninety down. We're in a gauntlet here, sir."

Kirk's comm buzzed. He looked down to see T'Laya's face on the screen. She looked upset.

"Are you okay?" asked Kirk with concern. "Is the computer bay functional?" He punched buttons, frustrated and feeling helpless. "All I can send you is a damned *Security* detail."

"I have to transport," she said calmly.

Confused, Kirk leaned to the comm. "I can't hear you," he said. "It's falling apart up here. My sensors are picking up a Romulan vessel, which makes no sense in this scenario. Something crazy is happening."

T'Laya leaned close to her vid screen.

"I'm transporting in five," she said.

"Transporting?" repeated Kirk.

"Shields at forty percent," reported McKenna.

Kirk checked his sensors. "Viktor, we're taking photon torpedoes from three different directions. Our destroyer screen is routed."

Tikhonov looked stunned. Damage reports were buzzing in from all decks.

"The *Valiant* is hailing us, sir," called Uhura.

"Open channel!" said Tikhonov angrily.

The face of Marla Kerrigan, a low-key, no-nonsense Command College cadet, appeared on the main viewscreen.

"This is Captain Kerrigan of the *Valiant*," she said in a brisk tone. "I've ordered a temporary cease-fire to give you a chance to explain your actions."

Viktor Tikhonov was arrogant enough, but when you added in his disdain for authoritative women, this was just too much.

"You launch a *surprise* attack on *both* of my flanks and

you want me to explain *my* actions?" he said, spitting as he spoke.

"Captain, your fighter wings are attacking our Gold embassy shuttle and laying waste to valuable stolen cargo that we're seeking to recover from the docking bay," replied Kerrigan. "I'll have to ask you to desist until we board and secure Zeta Starbase."

"Like hell I'll desist," said Tikhonov.

Then Kirk heard T'Laya again, right beside him.

She said: *I have to go now, Jim.*

He turned. But nobody was there. Then he frowned and looked down at the Security station comm screen. Nothing there, either.

"Great," he muttered. "Here goes my Heschl's Gyrus."

Help Viktor, she said. *Then come to the transporter bay.*

His eyes suddenly throbbing, Kirk put a hand to his forehead. It was happening again, yes, but he felt more lucid, more in control than before. He glanced at Lieutenant Caan, who stood next to McCoy at the Medical station. They were caught up in the drama on the bridge.

"That was another three torpedoes," called McKenna. "Shields at thirty percent!"

"Engineering, damage reports!" groaned Tikhonov.

Help him, said T'Laya again. *Hurry.*

Kirk slipped away from his Security station and then moved quickly to the command chair. He'd never seen

Tikhonov like this: frozen, indecisive. Beaten. He almost felt sorry for the bastard.

He leaned down quickly.

"Viktor, listen to me," he said.

Tikhonov gave him a haunted look. "We're dead, Kirk," he murmured.

"No, Viktor, we're not," said Kirk quietly. "There's a win-win situation here."

"I don't see it," said Tikhonov, shaking his head.

"Hail the *Valiant*," whispered Kirk. "Agree to the immediate cease-fire. Do it now! Offer to help secure their ambassador and let the Gold transports take all cargo, whatever they want, from Starbase Zeta. Let them have it, Viktor."

"Okay," said Tikhonov.

"Then hail the Nausicaans," said Kirk. "You may have noticed they're veteran pilots kicking our ass *and* Kerrigan's ass. Find out what *they* want. Be tough, but fair. Why are they holding the Gold ambassador? Is it just ransom, or something more? Find out! Because today your objective is to save Titan from disaster, *not punish pirates or humiliate the Romulans*."

Tikhonov gave him an odd look. "What Romulans?"

"I meant Gold fleet," Kirk said quickly. He clapped a hand on Viktor's shoulder. "Only *you* can pull this off, Viktor. You're the man."

He took a step back.

Tikhonov spun to Uhura. "Communications!" he shouted. "Hail the *Valiant* bridge, please."

Kirk turned, then went straight to the turbo lift.

She stood on a transporter pad.

When Kirk approached, she dropped to one knee and buried her face in her hands. He knelt too and took her by the shoulders.

"So it was you," he said.

"Part of it," she said, nodding. She wouldn't show her face.

"But why?" he asked.

"For peace," she said.

Kirk slid his fingers up her neck and into her hair.

"But it was wrong," she said. "It was hurting you. Even if it worked, it was wrong."

"Why me?" he asked.

Now T'Laya looked at him. Her eyes were liquid gray. She slid a small data cube into his hand.

"This will explain everything," she said.

Kirk held onto her.

"You can't just go," he said.

She smiled sadly. "They're on to me. If I stay, I'll end up in a Federation prison," she said. "Or worse."

Kirk glanced over at the transporter chief, Ensign Beck. The woman sat at the console, smiling off into space. She was clearly infected. T'Laya was thorough.

"She looks happy," he said.

"The coordinates are locked in," said T'Laya. "In all this ridiculous Zeta insanity, the signature of one small, cloaked Romulan science vessel won't be noticed until we're gone."

"But I already noticed," he said.

"Yes, you did," she replied. "Good sensors."

"So where are you going?" asked Kirk.

"In my training," said T'Laya, "Nverinn didn't prepare me for this sort of thing."

"Who is Nverinn? And prepare you for what . . . fraternizing with the enemy?"

T'Laya shook her head. "We never saw you as the enemy," she said. "But then, we never saw you as the spy's first love, either."

Kirk didn't know what to say.

T'Laya kissed him lightly on the cheek, then took a step back onto the transporter pad. As she did, the turbo-lift door whooshed open and Samarra Caan stepped out. She leveled a phaser at T'Laya.

"You're under arrest," she called.

As Kirk spun to face Caan, T'Laya calmly knelt back down on the pad.

"Lieutenant Caan," she said. She held up her right

hand. It formed a sign: two crossed fingers touching the tip of her thumb.

At this, Caan slowly lowered the weapon. *"Farr Jolan,"* she said.

T'Laya nodded. Tears rolled down her cheeks.

"Peace awaits," she said. Then to Kirk she said: "I do love you, Kirk. Remember tonight, when you look up at Gemini."

"I will," said Kirk.

T'Laya closed her eyes and said: "Energize."

Ensign Beck happily disassembled her into a matter stream of subatomic particles, fed her into a pattern buffer, and sent her away.

Kirk stared at the empty platform. Then he turned to Samarra.

"She's gone." He felt phaser-stunned.

"I'm sorry," said Samarra.

Kirk pointed at the platform.

"You let her go," Kirk said, looking at her in amazement.

"If only I had gotten here moments sooner," she replied, looking Kirk levelly in the eyes.

"Your secret is safe with me," he said. "I couldn't bear the idea of her in jail."

Kirk and Lieutenant Caan stood in silence for a moment, then Kirk spoke.

"What . . . was that sign she made?" he asked.

Lieutenant Caan holstered her phaser. "*Farr Jolan* is the sign of the Jolan peace movement," she said.

"Is it Romulan?" he asked.

"Yes," she replied. "We've heard that many Romulan scientists and intellectuals belong to the movement. Their goal is to avoid another war with Earth." She gave Kirk a look. "Imagine that."

Kirk nodded. This conversation was over for now.

Then he glanced at the ceiling and asked: "What's going on upstairs?"

Lieutenant Caan smiled. "Zeta Day One is over," she said. "So far, everybody won."

Kirk smiled. "Good job, Viktor."

"Yes," said Samarra. "He followed your advice to the letter."

Kirk frowned. "What are you talking about?"

Caan smiled slyly. She plucked the lieutenant commander rank insignia pin off Kirk's uniform shirt and bent it to reveal a surveillance wire. Then she lifted her hair to reveal the earpiece in her left ear.

"You . . . *bugged* me?" asked Kirk.

"When I put somebody under surveillance," she said, "I do it properly, Mr. Kirk."

CH.13.13
Gemini Rising

Senator Tashal watched the *Wasp* gunboat land. Unlike her shuttle, it was an imposing military craft. But when the Praetor emerged, he was alone. Her own head of security, Merak, looked surprised. Tashal smiled. She moved across the Center's docking bay to greet the head of the Romulan state.

"Welcome," she said.

"This is quite a place," said the Praetor, looking around.

"It is well-funded."

"I'll say."

As they moved down the corridor to the same glass-domed atrium where Senator Tashal had lunched with Nverinn just days earlier, Merak followed. But when they reached the dome's crystalline security door, Tashal turned to her guard.

"The Praetor and I will speak alone, Merak," she said.

"I am tasked with your protection," said Merak with a quick bow. In other words: *no.*

The Praetor, a short man—*so many powerful men are not tall,* thought Tashal—slid a small tablet pad from his tunic and tapped in a code. Then he turned it toward the security chief.

"This is a writ of imperial immunity," said the Praetor, showing the pad to Merak. "It extends to your entire team as well."

For a moment it appeared Merak would not back down. But the Praetor's look convinced him otherwise. After another quick bow he spun abruptly, marching back across the docking bay. They watched him go.

"That's how you reveal Tal Shiar people," said the Praetor with an amused gleam. "They hate the writ. Works every time."

Tashal smiled. She had long suspected that her state-assigned "security detail" served a dual purpose. Tal Shiar secret police had become less thuggish about spying on senators over the past century, but they could still be dangerous when thwarted.

She led the Praetor into Nverinn's garden patio.

"My god, it's lovely in here," he said, admiring the view.

"I chose this place for a reason," said Tashal.

"I imagine it inspires . . . *frank* dialogue," he said.

She nodded. "Nverinn was a master of many things,"

she said. "One of them was privacy." She glanced up. "This dome is a magnetized quasicrystal lattice. Only Nverinn knows how it works. But it has some sort of diffraction pattern that blocks any type of surveillance. We have our own soundproof room."

"Fascinating fellow," said the Praetor with a nod. "Too bad we lost him, Senator."

Tashal smiled sadly. "But he's still with us," she said after a moment.

As they both sat at the table under the willowy tree, the Praetor replied, "Really?"

Senator Tashal produced her own tablet pad and inserted a tiny data cube. Nverinn's face appeared on the display. He looked both haunted and amused, a complex jumble of emotion, even for a Romulan.

"Hello, friend," he said. "As always, this message is encoded for ionic dissolution. It will self-destruct, molecule by molecule, as it plays. So I hope you listen carefully."

Tashal exchanged a glance with the Praetor, who nodded in admiration.

"As you hear this, I have been either assassinated or I've warped light-years away," he said. "A fugitive to be hunted by the Tal Shiar for the rest of my life. It's a romantic notion, isn't it?"

Tashal smiled. Yes, it was.

"Let me clarify a few things," said Nverinn. "First my

Gemini agent at Starfleet Academy has been . . . well, *deconstructed*. The code will not trace back to the Star Empire. You are safe. However, I did not terminate T'Laya. She will join us shortly."

Tashal uttered a light murmur of relief.

"Forgive my weakness," Nverinn continued. "Her father, the great Vulcan ambassador, was a friend and ally to our cause, as you know. I swore I would consider his daughters as my own."

Here, the young girl, Majal, leaned into the camera's view and gave a quick grin. Nverinn chuckled and gently guided her back off-camera.

Tashal felt a warm sadness infuse her.

Nverinn continued: "Second, Gemini has always been an instrument of peace, not war or even espionage. I'm sure you suspected as much—I *hope* you did, anyway. Proclivity is genetic—you can be born with aggressive, warlike tendencies—but the brain is plastic. It is malleable. It can be programmed for peace."

The Praetor smiled grimly. "Tell that to the Tal Shiar," he said.

"Third," continued Nverinn, "our Vulcan connection continues to flourish. Sympathizers gain strength, and I predict that the Vulcan-Romulan reunification movement will one day join our Jolan peace movement. Such a bond would be a powerful one. Based on data from Gemini, I've come to believe that Humans and Vulcans, despite their considerable cultural differences, are attracted to one another at some very fundamental level. I've seen the evidence of this."

He paused to let his statement wash over his audience. And then he continued. "The same may be true of Humans and Romulans. So reunification would be a powerful weapon for peace in the galaxy."

"Weapons for peace," mumbled the Praetor. "I like that."

Now Nverinn leaned toward the camera.

"And fourth," he said, "you should know that I have agents now active in both the Military High Command and Tal Shiar. So the Gemini Project lives on." He smiled. "For all you know, the person sitting next to you may be infected."

Tashal and the Praetor exchanged another look. The Praetor grinned.

Finally, Nverinn bowed warmly—a familiar gesture—and said, "The final thing I wish to clarify is that I am missing you already."

And the message ended. The data cube glowed briefly. When Senator Tashal removed it from her tablet, the cube was warm.

The Praetor placed his hand on Tashal's arm.

"*Farr Jolan*, Senator," he said.

She nodded, wiping a delicate rivulet of tears from her cheek.

They sat in silence for quite a while.

A few light-years away, Kirk and McCoy sat on a bench across from the Academy Shuttle Hangar. A steady stream of cadets returning from Starbase 1 poured out of the facility, both exhilarated and exhausted from two days of Zeta.

McCoy rested his elbows on his knees. "Good god, I hate shuttle rides," he said.

Kirk was leaning back, staring up at the sky.

"I miss her already," he said.

McCoy glanced at him. "Listen, Jim," he said. "Samarra wants to check out some godforsaken sushi place over on Divisadero. Please join us."

Kirk smiled. "I thought you hated sushi."

"I do," said McCoy. "I'm from Mississippi, for god's sake. But if you're there, I can slip you my tuna rolls under the table."

"Okay," said Kirk.

McCoy stood up. "We'll pick you up in about forty-five minutes."

Kirk nodded.

McCoy shifted from foot to foot, then jumped up and

down a couple of times. "Feel that solid earth underfoot," he said.

Kirk grinned as McCoy strode off toward the Medical College.

Another group of cadets poured out of the Shuttle Hangar exit. He recognized Marla Kerrigan, the *Valiant* captain. She'd done a great job. A budding Starfleet star. When she saw Kirk, she gave him a wave.

"Nice job, Kirk," she called.

"You too," he replied.

"Very clever deployment on day two," she said. "You had me coming and going."

Kirk waved this away. "Viktor did a great job," he replied.

"Right," said Kerrigan dryly. A few cadets with her laughed at this as they strolled away.

Kirk leaned back again and stared up at the Gemini twins.

T'Laya's data cube explained a few things, but not everything. He understood how the neural code affected his brain. He understood its attempts to essentially duplicate his neocortex and his personal history, to create a kind of digital doppelganger of James T. Kirk for study. No harm was meant. Just research.

But she kept referring to herself *and* the code as Gemini, as if they were somehow one and the same. That, he didn't understand.

"We wanted to grasp Human psychology at the most fundamental level," she said. "But we went too far. We tried to mess with your wiring, trying to create an irresistible compulsion to seek creative, peaceful solutions in moments of conflict." Then she looked at the camera with those shining gray eyes and said: "But as it turned out, you didn't need rewiring. Those compulsions were already there."

When the data cube self-destructed, Kirk realized that his only trace of T'Laya's existence was gone. And so now he stared up at Pollux and Castor, the Gemini twins, and saw the constellation's outline in the sky.

"Mr. Kirk?" said a voice.

Kirk looked over. "Ah, Mr. Chekov," he said with a grin.

"Can I join you?"

"Please do," replied Kirk.

The young Russian plopped down on the bench. They sat in silence for a moment, watching a gaggle of female cadets bounce out of the hangar, bursting with bright energy. Then Chekov turned to Kirk.

"I have a question," he said.

"Shoot."

"When did you first kiss a girl?"

Kirk thought. "I was twelve," he said. "No, eleven." He rubbed his chin. "Well . . . depending on how you technically define a 'kiss.'"

"Oy, *horosho*," Chekov said and sighed, looking forlorn.

Kirk grinned. He pointed up at the sky.

"It'll happen, kid," he said. "Just keep your eye on those two bright stars up there. They're good luck."

"Castor and Pollux?" asked Chekov, gazing up. "Ay, my favorites. I like to draw a mental line from the Pleiades star cluster in Taurus right through Regulus there, the brightest star in Leo." He drew a line in the air. "See? That cuts *right* through the ecliptic."

Kirk stared at him. "This theoretical first girl?" he said. "She'd better be an incredible geek."

Chekov's eyes suddenly gleamed.

"Ay," he said. "I hope so."

Turn the page for a peek at another book in the Starfleet Academy series:

THE DELTA ANOMALY

CH.1.12
Fogbound

In the summer of 2255, the San Francisco fog was like a living entity. Pushed ashore by ocean winds, it would creep and crawl over the city's famous hills like a great white leviathan. Most nights that July, the city was smothered in the fog's wet hide. Twirling white tendrils drifted down streets and alleys.

But if you could get *above* the fog layer, it was a breathtaking view.

At eight hundred fifty feet aboveground, the woman bound and gagged in the beacon cone at the top of the Transamerica Pyramid was *well* above the fog.

It was a breathtaking experience—quite literally.

Jacqueline Madkins—Jackie to her friends—was a tough gal. From her sensible shoes to her sensible haircut, she radiated a no-nonsense air that had served her well in her career. She'd been running security operations in the famous 286-year-old pyramid, the crown jewel of the San Francisco skyline, for almost ten years. She was one of only four people in the world with unrestricted access to the beacon cone.

So when SecureCam Omega went offline earlier that night, she'd groaned in disbelief.

Jackie was alone in the security control center on the thirtieth floor. Her security team, a crew of twenty guards, was making its regular rounds. It was quite an operation. She sat at a bank of monitors flickering live feeds from the building's one hundred sixty surveillance cameras. She started tapping SecureCam Omega's feed button on the camera control console.

Blank screen. It was as if the camera went dead, but Jackie knew that couldn't happen. She shuddered involuntarily as a strange chill ran down her spine.

The top two hundred twelve feet of the Transamerica Pyramid was a hollow, translucent lumenite spire. Inside the spire, a steep staircase zigzagged up to the cone that housed the one-thousand-watt LED aviation warning light, a flashing red strobe. SecureCam Omega—the one that was apparently on the blink—surveyed the beacon chamber. Getting to it was a long, hard climb.

Jackie thought about that climb and looked down rue-fully at her feet. "It's not that I don't like fabulous shoes," she'd recently explained to her sister, Dawn, "it's just that they are not exactly practical in my line of work!"

Suddenly, her comlink buzzed. She hit a button on her belt unit.

"Talk to me, Will," she said.

"Did you just *see* that?" blurted the voice of Will Rosen, one of her night-team guards. He was just a teenager, and he sounded shaken.

"See what?" asked Jackie.

"The flash!" cried Will.

Jackie swiveled her chair to another console and checked what she called "the big board," a full schematic of the entire building. Blue glowing icons marked the real-time locations of all twenty team members. Each icon was numbered.

"Okay, I got you marked up on forty-eight," she said. "Is that right?"

The Transamerica Pyramid's entire forty-eighth floor was a single, spectacular conference room. It offered a full 360-degree view of the city.

"Confirmed," said Will. "It was, like, right outside the window." His breathing was short and shallow. "Very bright, like an explosion."

"I didn't hear anything," replied Jackie.

"Neither did I," said Will.

"This is getting really weird," Jackie muttered.

"What's that?" asked Will.

Now her red line was ringing. This was a direct emergency hotline to SFPD. "Nothing. Sit tight, Will. I'll be right up," she said, and cut off the comlink. Then she picked up the red receiver on the console. "Pyramid security, this is Madkins." She spoke with professional calm.

"Yo, Jackie, you okay over there?" said a voice on the line.

"Hey, Sam," she said. It was Sergeant Sam Kalar at SFPD's central district station, just down the street. "What's up?"

"We got people reporting a big lightning strike on the pyramid," replied the voice. "Calls coming in left and right."

"One of my guys saw a flash, but no sound," said Jackie. "I think we're fine. I've got power, all systems running. But we'll check it out."

"Okay," said Sergeant Kalar. "Let me know."

"Roger," she said, and hung up.

Time for my workout, she thought grimly.

● · ∴ ✦ · ✦ ·∴ ·

Fifteen minutes later, Jackie was still lumbering up the spire staircase. She was in good shape, but this was the equivalent of climbing a twenty-one-story spiraling fire escape. After a few rest stops, she finally reached the landing that supports the final twenty-foot ladder leading up to the beacon platform.

"Going in," she said into her comlink.

"I got you marked, boss," came the voice of Will.

Jackie slowly hauled herself up the ladder through a narrow opening into the small cone-shaped room. A glass pyramid cap at the top housed the Halo3000 aviation warning beacon. The red strobe flashed forty times per minute with an intensity of twenty thousand candelas, bright enough to cause retinal damage. But a shield platform underneath the beacon let Jackie scan the chamber without danger.

"No damage up here," she said over the comlink, an obvious note of relief in her voice.

"Copy that," said Will.

Then Jackie spotted the malfunctioning camera near the floor. With a simple twist, the unit clicked off of its base. She tucked it into a side pouch she'd worn for just this purpose.

Nothing to worry about, she told herself, allowing relief to wash over her. She mentally chastised herself for having felt so worried over nothing.

As she approached the ladder for descent, a slight hissing sound from above caught her attention. She glanced up at the beacon's shield platform. Wisps of black were slowly drifting downward.

"What the . . . ," she said.

"What's that, boss?" called Will.

"I see smoke up here," she said, puzzled. "Up in the beacon housing."

She listened to crackling silence over the comlink. Will was as perplexed as she was. "We'd better get a repair guy up here ASAP," she said. "There's a number in the database for Aviation Safety Systems. Call right now and, oh my god . . ."

Black smoke was now pouring into the chamber from above. It shot down in three long plumes. Each plume started circling Jackie and tightening its spiral. She could feel the smoke slithering over her bare arms, face, and throat. The last things she felt before falling unconscious were the distinct sensation of a powerful pressure strapping her arms to her sides, and a thin film spreading across her mouth, sealing it shut.

"Jackie, do you read me?" called Will over the comlink. "Jackie?"

Jackie couldn't reply. Moments later, she lost consciousness.

CH.2.12
The Delta Quadrant

Starfleet Academy life was grueling.

Weeks of rigorous, unending study. Physical and mental training that no sport could prepare you for. Brutal hours in the tactical simulators, followed by humiliating debriefing sessions filled with failure analyses. And then there was the competition—the finest minds and bodies in the entire galaxy, pitted against one another daily, *hourly*. It took a toll.

The Starfleet cadets needed to blow off steam.

Chestnut Street in San Francisco—where the beautiful people and aliens prowled, mated, and dated—was a favorite hangout. Tonight the city's infamous fog swirled like a pale fluid. James T. Kirk, Leonard "Bones" McCoy, and a Tellarite cadet named Glorak strolled down Chestnut Street looking for fun while trying to avoid collisions. Visibility was low. The fog was so thick that bodies appeared and disappeared like ghosts—for example, that Chinese lady carrying a huge, live lobster.

"Good god!" said McCoy, jumping out of the way.

Kirk laughed and watched the woman pass. The lobster was waving its rubber-banded claws like a symphony conductor. Kirk pointed at the crustacean. "I'll see you at dinner, Bernstein!" he called. A few steps later the apparition melted back into the white mist and disappeared.

Glorak wrinkled his piglike snout and said, "Your oceans produce such strange creatures!"

"Don't get me started on oceans," grumbled McCoy.

Kirk turned to Glorak. "Bones hates oceans worse than he hates space," he explained.

"You . . . hate space?" asked Glorak.

"Yes, I hate space," said McCoy.

"Interesting that you've chosen a career with Starfleet, Dr. McCoy," said Glorak.

"Oh, is it?" said McCoy testily.

Kirk slung an arm around McCoy's shoulders. "'Space is disease and danger wrapped in darkness and silence.' I believe that's an exact quote." Kirk blinked up at a neon sign glowing in the fog. "First words you ever spoke to me, Bones. Kinda makes me nostalgic."

McCoy glared at Kirk. "Nostalgic for what?"

"For simpler days," said Kirk. "For . . . innocence."

"One thing you've *never* been, Jim," said McCoy, "is innocent."

Kirk whacked McCoy on the back. "Speaking of which . . . let's find girls. I hear they tend to flock in this vicinity."

McCoy shook his head. "I can't even find the damned sidewalk."

"I warned you about that Andorian ale, my friend," said Glorak darkly.

"I'm talking about the *fog*, for god's sake," said McCoy.

"Oh," said Glorak.

"Come on," said Kirk. "Let's find that new club."

Word around campus was that a holo-karaoke bar had just opened off Chestnut. It was called the Delta Quadrant, and rumor had it that some female cadets were planning a birthday outing there that evening. Kirk despised karaoke, especially this new version where you could sing your song surrounded by holographic projections of the actual band. But, Kirk loved female cadets. So it was an acceptable trade-off, tactically speaking.

The three cadets continued up Chestnut, dodging loud groups of bar-hopping pedestrians. Kirk stopped a few people to ask directions to the Delta Quadrant, but everyone he encountered was either a little too drunk—or too eager to get home with that evening's conquest—to stop and give clear directions. So the trio kept getting lost down side streets. As usual, Kirk pushed ahead of the others.

"I'm making poor command decisions," he muttered to himself. Glancing down a dark alley, he spotted several dark entities twirling in the whitish fog. He stopped to watch, mesmerized. Their jerky movements seemed inhuman. Odd, hissing voices wafted toward Kirk, and a chill seized him. But then the entities suddenly evaporated. The figures literally melted away into the fog.

When the others caught up, Kirk pointed down the alley. "Did you see that?"

"See what?" asked McCoy.

"Creepy people dancing and, like, . . . hissing," said Kirk.

Glorak snorted loudly. "You sure they were *dancing*, Kirk?"

McCoy glared at Glorak. "I hate it when you suck in your snout like that," he said.

Glorak smiled at McCoy and sucked in his snout a few more times.

"Yes, that's it exactly," McCoy said, disgusted.

Kirk stared into the fog. The vision had been unsettling. After a few more seconds, he shrugged. "Whatever."

Kirk, McCoy, and Glorak pushed ahead through the night's white shroud. As they turned the next corner they heard loud music pulsing from an open doorway just ahead.

Above the door, a 3-D holograph of the Greek letter delta hovered in the air, spinning eerily in the fog.

"Ah, that must be it!" cried Glorak.

As Kirk rolled into the club, he expertly scoped out the room. Within moments, his eyes settled on the lovely Cadet Uhura, sitting at a corner table with the voluptuous, red-haired, green-skinned Gaila. Kirk smiled—this was a triple score. First, like all good Orion girls, Cadet Gaila *loved* men. Second, Gaila was a computer lab tech, and it always paid to be on good terms with someone who had access to Starfleet guts. And third . . . well, one of Kirk's favorite pastimes was trying to make the straight-laced Cadet Uhura uncomfortable. She was absolutely adorable when she squirmed.

"Gentlemen, lock your targets," said Kirk.

"Right," said McCoy. "Every man for himself."

"Standard rules of engagement?" asked Glorak.

"Correct, Mr. Glorak," replied Kirk. "Rendezvous here at 2200 hours."

"But Mr. Kirk, that's curfew!" said Glorak.

Kirk nodded. "Good point, Mr. Glorak," he said. "Make it 2155."

"That leaves little room for error."

Kirk glanced over at Uhura and Gaila. "I don't anticipate errors," he said, grinning.

Kirk moved across the room like a man with a mission. He passed the club stage where a wobbly Andorian girl with white hair and fishnet tights was making a fool of herself singing an ancient Madonna song. She blew Kirk a kiss as he passed. As he approached Uhura, Kirk was disappointed to see that his fun had been compromised: She looked to be already uncomfortable, and it wasn't because of him. Next to her, Gaila loudly ordered another drink that she clearly didn't need.

"Hello, Cadets!" said Kirk brightly.

"Jim Kirk!" shrieked Gaila. She pointed at him. "Look! It's that Jim Kirk!"

Uhura nodded. "So it is."

"He's hot!" she whisper-yelled to Uhura. Gaila then exploded into a honking laugh that sounded like alarmed waterfowl rising from a lake. The noise was so frightening that Kirk nearly backed away.

"Wow," said Kirk, nodding. "Impressive *levity* there."

"S'my birthday," slurred Gaila. She attempted to lean seductively toward Kirk and almost fell off her stool. "Where's my gift, Jim Kirk?" She grabbed a handful of his shirt. "Is it in your pocket?"

"Oh, well, see, I didn't . . . ," began Kirk, but Gaila cut

him off by waving wildly at a passing cocktail waitress.

"One more!" she screamed over the thumping music. "Right here! Green drink for green girl!" She pointed at herself, laughing hysterically.

The waitress glided in close. She said, "I already *got* your order, hon. But are you sure you want it?"

"I think it's a poor decision, Gaila," said Uhura.

"Excellent!" said Gaila. She looked up at Kirk. "I'm excellent."

"I can see that."

"You're a little *too* excellent, Gaila," said Uhura.

Nearby, the bartender slung a slushy green drink onto the service stand. As the waitress hustled off to snag it, Gaila suddenly slid off her chair and onto the floor at Kirk's feet. She started giggling uncontrollably.

"Whoooops!" she howled.

People at the next table laughed, but looked a little uneasy.

"Wow," said Kirk. "You're *really* hammered."

"Thank you!"

As Kirk helped Gaila back onto her chair, she flung her arms tightly around his neck. Kirk was momentarily tempted, but then he caught a look from Uhura—a cross between "Don't you dare!" and "Please god, help me!" So he unlocked himself from Gaila's grip and shot off to intercept the cocktail waitress.

"I've got this," he said, dropping money on her tray and snagging the drink.

"Don't give it to green girl," said the waitress wearily.

Kirk nodded and quickly slipped the drink to a stocky, jovial Xannon cadet named Braxim at the next table.

"On the house," said Kirk.

Braxim smiled broadly. "Thank you, Mr. Kirk," he said.

"Don't mention it." Kirk leaned down. "And I mean that literally."

Braxim laughed heartily. "I have been watching the Orion girl," he said, beating his chest for emphasis as Xannons do. "You will need assistance, I am sure. Orion girls can be *most* unruly. Trust me—I know firsthand."

"Thanks, friend," said Kirk, making a mental note to ask for more information on that firsthand knowledge sometime.

When Kirk returned to the table, Uhura was trying to convince Gaila to head back to the Presidio, the site of the Starfleet Academy campus. But the Orion girl abruptly jumped to her feet and, without a word, staggered off to the restroom.

Uhura gave Kirk a dark look. "As much as it pains me to say this to you, of all people," she said, "I need some help."

"Okay," said Kirk.

"I doubt this girl can walk all the way back to campus,"

said Uhura. "Let's drag her to the Powell Street shuttle. It's just a few blocks."

Kirk nodded. "For a price," he said.

Uhura narrowed her eyes. "Are you kidding?"

"Just tell me your first name," said Kirk, smiling at her in a way that made most girls swoon.

Annoyingly, Uhura just stared at him.

"So . . . no deal?" asked Kirk. Uhura rolled her eyes and started after Gaila. "Okay, well, I'll help you anyway," called Kirk as she hurried away, "whatever your name is." As Uhura ducked into the restroom without responding, he added: "I'll be waiting right here, sweetheart."

Kirk spotted McCoy nearby and quickly pulled the doctor away from a few prospective "patients." "We need to escort Uhura and Gaila to the shuttle landing," he said quickly.

"Why?" asked McCoy. "It's just four blocks away. And you're kind of interrupting something here," he said, motioning discreetly to a cute blonde sipping a pink drink.

Kirk winked at her. She winked back. *Focus,* he told himself.

"It's foggy out," replied Kirk. "Dangerous."

"Are you joking?" exclaimed McCoy. "These women are Starfleet-trained in self-defense, Jim! They can handle themselves just fine."

"I know that," says Kirk. "But Gaila is messed up, bad. Uhura needs help getting her back to the dorm."

"Good god, Jim, I'm a doctor, not a babysitter," said McCoy, his eyes returning to linger on the blonde.

"Some medical skills *might* be useful here," said Kirk.

"That girl doesn't need my skills."

Kirk grabbed McCoy's jacket. "Look, I need you, Bones," he said. "This Orion woman scares the hell out of me."

McCoy grinned. "Well, *that's* a first."

"And I think we'll need a couple more guys," said Kirk, scanning the club.

Ten minutes later, Glorak and Braxim stood with Kirk and McCoy near the door to the women's restroom.

Tellarites and Xannons were both stout, strong races, so this duo was a nice addition to the escort detail. And Braxim, like most Xannons, was a fun-loving fellow who loved company. With his big barrel chest and bony forehead protrusion, he seemed to be forever leaning forward.

"I love nights such as tonight!" he exclaimed, giving his chest a quick thump. "I find coastal fog to be most bracing and romantic, particularly when it lacks a methane component!"

McCoy nodded. "Yes, methane fog does put a damper on romance," he agreed.

Suddenly Uhura burst from the women's room, alone. "Did she come out?" she asked, frowning.

"Gaila?" asked Kirk. "No."

"Are you sure?"

Kirk looked around. "We've been here ten minutes or so," he said. "When did you see her last?"

"Just a minute ago," she said. "She was in a stall. I went out to wash my hands, and then she was gone." Uhura ducked back into the restroom, then popped back out.

"The window's open!" she said angrily.

"Crap. Let's go," said Kirk.

The five cadets hustled to the club entrance. "Bones, you check any alleys around the club with Glorak," said Kirk quickly. "Braxxy and I will head up to Chestnut. She can't be far." He turned to Uhura. "You should stay here in case she comes back looking for you."

"Oh, she won't," said Uhura with irritation, stepping outside and scanning the foggy sidewalk. "She's on the prowl. I've seen Gaila like this before. She's *relentless*."

"I fear for the men of this city," muttered McCoy.

"She is *quite* inebriated," said Braxim, squinting out at the fog. "How far could she go?"

Kirk looked at McCoy.

"Pretty far," they said simultaneously.

The cadets split into two search parties—the result of good Starfleet away-team tactical training. McCoy, Uhura, and Glorak deployed toward the Powell Street shuttle landing, four blocks up Russian Hill—a steep climb. Meanwhile, Kirk and the brawny Braxim started tracking up and down Marina District streets. A sudden inland gust churned up the milky fog around them. It drifted in jagged tendrils, seeming almost alive.

"Still like the fog, Braxxy?" asked Kirk, wiping his eyes.

Braxim smiled wryly. "It does seem unfriendly now," he admitted.

Kirk pointed to an old-fashioned neon sign, PAK'S GROCERY, glimmering on the corner just ahead. "Your turn," he said. "I'll scout ahead a bit."

As Braxim ducked into the store to search for Gaila, Kirk moved along the street looking for alleys.

Suddenly, he heard Gaila. She was singing.

"Gaila!" he called out. "Yo, girl!"

Kirk followed the sound to the entrance of an alley running behind some classic row houses. Abruptly, the singing stopped . . . replaced by a hissing metallic voice. Now Kirk heard Gaila gasping. He ran up the alley until he could see a vague outline of Gaila with another murky figure, dark in the pale fog, wrapped like a black cloak around her. He hesitated for a brief moment, wondering if he was interrupting something. Was Gaila gasping or *choking*?

Kirk decided she was probably not enjoying the encounter. She sounded like she was convulsing. If he was wrong, he'd deal with it. He had to make sure Gaila wasn't in trouble.

"Hey!" shouted Kirk. "Hey, *you!*"

As Kirk shouted, the figure that had been all over Gaila reared up—huge now, maybe seven feet tall. The hissing morphed into a familiar sound, but Kirk couldn't place it. Kirk shouted again, using his "command voice" (learned in Fleet Command and Control Methods) but the dark entity did not move.

Then Gaila groaned in agony. Now Kirk was pissed.

He dropped low, lunged, then sidestepped and unleashed a jab kick. He was sure he had a clean, easy shot at the attacker, but his foot struck nothing but air. Suddenly he was locked in a vise grip. The guy was incredibly strong. Kirk couldn't move his arms. Then it got worse—fast. He felt a sticky sheet being pulled over his head. The sheet tightened across his face. He couldn't move, and he couldn't breathe.

Then Braxim burst through the fog.

"I called the police!" he shouted at the attacker, holding up his open hand-held communicator. "I called 911!"

Suddenly the sheet peeled off of Kirk's face. He fell to the ground, gasping for air, and looked up to see the fog rolling toward Braxim's feet.

In an impossibly deep voice, the entity spoke a phrase in a language that Kirk did not recognize. He seemed to be speaking to Braxim.

Then the attacker completely melted away into the thick fog.